GATH

Planet Gath is a cruel, harsh place visited only as an intergalactic tourist attraction for its annual storm season. But then, *they* come: Dumarest — a man with a strange past and a threatening future; the old Matriarch of the planet Kund with her ward Seena Thoth; the dangerous cyber Dyne and the Prince of Emmened — a sadist, with his fearful followers . . . And, according to legend, in the eerie storms which sweep the mountains of Gath, the dead arise and speak . . .

E. C. TUBB

GATH

Complete and Unabridged

LINFORD
Leicester

First published in Great Britain

First Linford Edition
published 2010

British Library CIP Data

Tubb, E. C.
  Gath. - - (Linford mystery library)
  1. Science fiction.
  2. Large type books.
  I. Title II. Series
  823.9'14–dc22

ISBN 978–1–44480–031–9

01 | 16

Published by
F. A. Thorpe (Publishing)
Anstey, Leicestershire

Set by Words & Graphics Ltd.
Anstey, Leicestershire
Printed and bound in Great Britain by
T. J. International Ltd., Padstow, Cornwall

This book is printed on acid-free paper

1

He woke counting seconds, rising through interminable strata of ebon chill to warmth, light and a growing awareness. At thirty-two the eddy currents had warmed him back to normal. At fifty-eight his heart began beating under its own power. At seventy-three the pulmotor ceased helping his lungs. At two hundred and fifteen the lid swung open with a pneumatic hiss.

He lay enjoying the euphoria of resurrection.

It was always the same this feeling of wellbeing. Each time he woke there was the surge of gladness that once again he had beaten the odds. His body tingled with life after the long sleep during which it had been given the opportunity to mend minor ills. The waking drugs stimulated his imagination. It was pleasant to lie, eyes closed, lost in the pleasure of the moment.

'You okay?'

The voice was sharp, anxious, breaking

into his mood. Dumarest sighed and opened his eyes. The light was too bright. He lifted a hand to shield his face, lowered it as something blocked the glare. Benson stood looking down at him from the foot of the open box. He looked the same as Dumarest remembered, a small man with a puckered face, an elaborate fringe of beard and a slick of black hair, but how much did a man have to age before it showed?

'You made it,' said the handler. He sounded pleased. 'I didn't expect trouble but for a minute back there you had me worried.' He leaned forward, his head blocking more of the light. 'You sure that you're okay?'

Dumarest nodded, reluctantly recognizing the need to move. Reaching out he clamped his hands on the edges of the box and slowly pulled himself upright. His body was, as expected, nude, bleached white, the skin tight over prominent bone. Cautiously he flexed his muscles, inflated the barrel of his chest. He had lost fat but little else. He was still numb for which he was thankful.

'I haven't lost a one yet,' boasted the handler. 'That's why you had me worried. I've got a clean score and I want it to stay that way.'

It wouldn't, of course. Benson was still fresh at the game. Give him time and he would become less conscientious, more and he would grow careless, finally he wouldn't give a damn. That's when some of his kind thought it cute to cut the dope and watch some poor devil scream his lungs raw with the agony of restored circulation.

'I'm forgetting,' he said. He passed over a cup of brackish water. Dumarest drank it, handed back the cup.

'Thanks.' His voice was thin, a little rusty. He swallowed and tried again. This time he sounded more like his normal self. 'How about some basic?'

'Coming right up.'

Dumarest sat hunched in the box as Benson crossed to the dispenser. He wrapped his arms about his chest, conscious of the cold, the bleakness of the compartment. The place resembled a morgue. A chill, blue-lit cavern, the air tainted with a chemical smell. A low place, shapeless with jutting struts and curved beams, harsh with the unrelieved monotony of unpainted metal.

There was no need for heat in this part of the ship and no intention of providing comfort. Just the bare metal, the ultraviolet lamps washing the naked, coffin-like boxes with their sterilizing glow. Here was where the livestock rode, doped, frozen, ninety per cent dead. Here was the steerage for travellers willing to gamble against the fifteen per cent mortality rate.

Such travel was cheap — its sole virtue.

But something was wrong.

Dumarest sensed it with the caution born of long years of experience. It wasn't the waking. He had gained awareness long before the end of the five-minute waking cycle. It wasn't Benson. It was something else. Something which should not be.

He found it after he had moistened the tips of his fingers and rested them lightly against the bare metal of the structure. They tingled with the faint but unmistakable effect of the Erhaft field. The ship was still in space.

And travellers were never revived until after landing.

Benson returned with a pint of basic. A thin vapour rose from the cup, scientifically designed to stimulate the appetite. He smiled as he passed it over.

'Here,' he said. 'Get this down while it's still warm.'

The fluid was sickly with glucose, laced with vitamins, thick with protein. Dumarest swallowed it with caution, taking small sips, careful of his stomach. He handed Benson the empty container and stepped from the box. A drawer beneath held his clothes and personal effects. He dressed and checked his gear.

'It's all there,' said Benson. His voice was hollow against the echoing metal. 'Everything's just as you left it.'

Dumarest tightened his belt and stamped his feet in their boots. They were good boots. A wise traveller looked after his feet.

'I wouldn't steal anything from you people.' The handler was insistent on his honesty. 'I don't blame you for checking your gear but I wouldn't steal it.'

'Not if you've got any sense,' agreed Dumarest. He straightened, towering over

5

the other man. 'But it's been tried.'

'Maybe. But not by me.'

'Not yet.'

'Not ever. I'd never do a thing like that.'

Dumarest shrugged, knowing better, then looked at the other boxes. He crossed to them, checking their contents. Three young bulls, two rams, a solid block of ice containing salmon, a dog, a plethora of cats — the general livestock cargo of any starship travelling at random and trading in anything which would yield a profit. Animals but no people — despite all the empty boxes. He looked at the handler.

'There were other travellers wanting passage at your last port of call,' he said evenly. 'Why only me?'

'You came early.'

'So?'

'We had a last-minute charter. The Matriarch of Kund and party. You were already in freeze or you'd have been dumped out with the other passengers and freight.' Benson crossed to the dispenser and refilled the empty cup.

'They took the whole ship.'

'Big money,' said Dumarest. The only way to break the Captain's bond was to buy off anyone who could claim prior right. 'Didn't she have a ship of her own?'

'She did,' Benson rejoined Dumarest. 'I heard one of our engineers talking and he said that their drive was on the blink. Anyway, the Old Man took the charter and we left right away.'

Dumarest nodded, taking his time over the second pint. A spaceman could live on four ounces of basic a day and he was beginning to feel bloated. Benson sat close, his eyes on the big man's face. He seemed eager to talk, to break the silence normal to his part of the ship. Dumarest humoured him.

'A matriarch, eh? Plenty of women to liven things up.'

'They're travelling High,' said Benson. 'All but the guards and they don't want to play.' He hunched even closer. 'What's it like being a traveller? I mean, what do you get out of it?'

His eyes were curious and something else. Dumarest had seen it so often before, the look of the stay-put to the mover-on. They all had it and the envy would grow. Then, as the prison of their ship began to close in, that envy would sour into hate. That's when a wise traveller waited for another ship.

'It's a way of life,' said Dumarest. 'Some like it, some don't. I do.'

'How do you go about it. What do you do between trips?'

'Look around, get a job, build another stake for passage to somewhere else.' Dumarest finished the basic and set down the empty cup. 'Broome is a busy world. I won't have too much trouble finding a ship heading for somewhere I haven't yet seen.' He caught the handler's expression.

'We're going to Broome? The place you told me was the next port of call?'

'No.' Benson retreated a little. Dumarest caught his arm.

'I booked for Broome,' he said coldly. His hand tightened. The handler winced. 'Did you lie?'

'No!' Benson had courage. 'You booked the usual,' he said. 'A passage to the next port of call. I thought it was Broome. It was Broome until we got that charter.'

'And now?'

'We're three days' flight from Gath.'

★ ★ ★

Close your eyes, hold your breath, concentrate. On Gath you can hear the music of the spheres!

So claimed the admen and they could have been telling the truth — Dumarest had never wanted to find out. Gath was for tourists with a two-way ticket. An 'attraction' with no home industry, no stable society in which a traveller could work to build the price of get-away fare. A dead, dumb, blind-alley world at the end of the line.

He stood at the edge of the field looking it over. The gravity was normal but that was all. Gath was old and kept one face turned continually towards the dying sun. There were no seasons, nothing to disturb the brooding stillness of the air but the periodic storms which, three times a year, tore and savaged the dreaming atmosphere. At such times the influence of its satellites co-joined to produce an oscillation of the planet on its axis. The resulting libration upset the delicate balance of thermodynamic distribution and, for a brief while, Gath became alive again. The storms were what the tourists came to see. The thing which had brought Dumarest unwillingly to Gath. He was not alone.

Down past the levelled area of the field, crouched in the shallow scoop of a valley running down to the sea, squatted a huddle of ramshackle dwellings. They reflected the poverty which hung over them like a miasma. They gave some shelter and a measure of privacy and that was all.

Further off and to one side, on some high ground well away from the danger of the field and the smell of the camp, sat a prim collection of prefabricated huts and inflatable tents. There sat the money and the comfort which money could provide. The tourists who travelled High, doped with quick-time so that a day seemed an hour, a week a day.

Those in the camp had travelled like Dumarest — Low. Those who rode Middle stayed with the ships which were their home. They would stay, so Benson had said, until after the storm. Then they would leave. Others would return for the next storm. On Gath that was about four months. An age.

Dumarest walked from the field, thrusting his way past a handful of men who stared at the ships with hopeless eyes, feeling his boots sink into the dirt as he left the hardened surface. It was hot, the air heavy, the humidity high. He opened his collar as he entered the camp. A narrow lane wound between the dwellings, uneven and thick with dust. It would lead, he knew, to a central area — common to all such encampments. He was looking for information. He found it sooner than he hoped.

A man sat before the open front of one of the dwellings. It had been clumsily built from scraps of discarded plastic sheeting supported by branches, weighted with rocks. The man was bearded, dirty, his clothing a shapeless mess. He stooped

11

over a boot trying to mend a gaping rip in the side. He looked up as Dumarest approached.

'Earl!' The boot and scraps of twisted wire fell aside as he sprang to his feet. 'Man, am I sorry to see you!'

'Megan!' Dumarest's eyes probed the dirt, the beard, the shapeless clothing. 'As bad as all that?'

'Worse.' Megan stooped, picked up his boot, swore as he thrust a finger through the hole. 'Just arrived?'

'Yes.'

'How was the handler on your ship?' Megan was too casual. 'A decent type?'

'Couldn't be better. Why?'

'Decent enough to trust a man?'

'He isn't a fool.' Dumarest sat down before the hut. 'You know the rules, Megan. No cash, no ride. How long have you been stuck here?'

'Over a year.' Viciously he flung down the damaged boot. 'Four times I've seen the ships come in and four times they've left without me. If I don't get away soon I won't be able to get away at all. Even now I'd be taking more than a normal risk.'

He was optimistic. Beneath the dirt Megan was gaunt, his clothes hanging from a skeletal frame. For him to travel Low in his condition was suicide. He looked enviously at Dumarest.

'You're looking fit,' he said, 'for a man who's just landed.'

'I had luck,' said Dumarest, and smiled at the memory. 'The handler stepped out of line and got himself disciplined. He woke me three days early for the sake of company. He wanted someone to talk to. I let him talk.'

'And got well fed for listening.' Megan scowled. 'I bet he wanted to know all about being a traveller.'

'You know?'

'It happens all the time. Damn yokels! They can't understand that it takes guts to operate on your own. They get to hate us for being what they can't and they vent their spite any way they can. Damn them all to hell!'

He sat down, lacking the strength for sustained anger.

'I got here by mistake,' he said quietly. 'A lying handler said the ship was bound for Largis. I didn't know he'd lied until I was outside the ship. At first I wasn't too worried. I'd heard about Gath and was curious. I wanted — well, never mind that. I even had a little money to tide me over before settling down to earn a stake. That's when it hit me.'

'No work,' said Dumarest. 'No loose money lying around. I know how it is.'

'You were always smart,' said Megan dully. 'I remember you talking about it that time on Schick. The worlds a traveller had to stay away from if he didn't want to get stranded. Well, what good did it do you?'

'None,' said Dumarest flatly. He explained how he came to be on the planet. Megan nodded, moodily examining his boot.

'I saw the party land. Big, well-armed, enough stuff to stock a store.'

'They've got money,' agreed Dumarest. 'Maybe they came here to hunt.'

'Then they're wasting their time.' Megan spat his disgust. 'There's no game

14

on this planet, and people don't visit Gath to hunt.'

'Then the guns must be for something else.' Dumarest was thoughtful. 'A big party, you say?'

'That's right. They didn't look like a bunch of tourists and didn't act like one. More like a military detachment than anything else. Female guards everywhere, tough as nails and as ugly as sin. They've set up their tents in Hightown.' Megan picked up the scraps of wire and began to fumble with his boot. His hands were shaking. 'I offered to carry some of their stuff. One of them pushed me aside. That's how I ripped my boot. I tripped and almost busted an ankle.' He pursed his lips. 'Nice people.'

'I know the type.' Dumarest reached out and took the boot and wire. 'Here, let me do that.'

Megan didn't object. He sat watching, trying to pluck up his courage. 'Earl. I — '

'Later,' said Dumarest quickly. 'After I've finished this you can show me where I can get us something to eat.' He didn't

15

look at the other man, concentrating on the repair. 'Now let me see,' he mused. 'The problem is to lash it tight enough not to yield but leave it flexible enough to give.'

But that wasn't the real problem.

2

There was no cycle of night and day on Gath. Always the swollen ball of the sun glowered over the horizon, tinting the leaden sea the colour of blood. To the east there was darkness, cold, mysterious. Between light and dark ran a strip of bearable temperature but only here, on this waterlogged world, did it touch both land and ocean. The accident of distribution had helped to make the planet unique.

'A dying world,' said a voice. It was soft, carefully modulated. 'Angered at the knowledge of its inevitable end. A little jealous, a little pathetic, very much afraid and most certainly cruel.'

'You are speaking of Gath?' Seena Thoth, ward of the Matriarch of Kund, stayed looking through the window set into the wall of the tent. There was no need for her to turn. She had recognized the voice. Synthosilk rustled as the tall figure of Cyber Dyne stepped to her side.

'What else, my lady?'

'I thought it possible you spoke in analogy.' She turned and faced the cyber. He wore the scarlet robe of his class, beneath its cowl his face was smooth, ageless, unmarked by emotion. 'The Matriarch is also old, perhaps a little afraid, most certainly cruel — to those who oppose her will.'

'To be a ruler is not an easy thing, my lady.'

'It can be worse to be a subject.' She turned from the window, her face pale beneath the black mound of lacquered hair. 'I saw one before we left Kund. A man impaled on a cone of polished glass. They told me that his sensitivity to pain had been heightened and that he would take a long time to die.'

'He was a traitor, my lady. The manner of his death was chosen so as to serve as an example to others who might be tempted to rebel.'

'By your advice?' She tightened her lips at the inclination of his head. 'So. You oppose rebellion?'

'I do not oppose. I do not aid. I take no sides. I advise. I am of value only while I remain detached.' He spoke his credo in the same soft, even modulation in which he would announce the arrival of battle, murder and sudden death.

She hid her repulsion as she heard it. It was instinctive, this dislike of hers for the cyber. As a woman she was proud of her sex and the power it gave. She liked to read desire in the eyes of men but she had never read it in the eyes of Dyne. She would never read it. No woman ever would.

At five he had been chosen. At fifteen, after a forced puberty, he had undergone an operation on the thalamus. He could feel no joy, no hate, no desire, no pain. He was a coldly logical machine of flesh and blood. A detached, dispassionate, human robot. The only pleasure he could know was the mental satisfaction of correct deduction.

'It seems to me,' she said slowly, 'that your logic is at fault. To make a martyr is a mistake. Martyrs make causes.'

'Not unless there is a cause to make,'

he corrected. 'The man was a paid assassin. He knew the risk he ran and accepted it. The opposition on Kund, my lady, is not of the masses. It is common knowledge that the rule of the Matriarch has been benevolent.'

'That is true.'

'It is also well known that she is no longer young and has still not named her successor.'

She nodded, impatient with him for labouring the obvious.

'That is why the site of the execution was chosen so carefully,' he murmured. 'It was no accident that the man was impaled before the residence of the Lady Moira.'

The suggestion was outrageous. Seena both knew and liked the woman. 'You say that she would employ an assassin? Ridiculous!'

Dyne remained silent.

'The Lady Moira is rich and powerful,' she admitted. 'But she is a woman of honour.'

'Honour, my lady, can mean many things to many people.'

'But assassination — '

'Is an accepted political instrument. It is feared that the Matriarch is no longer at her prime. There are those who are concerned about the succession. That,' he added, 'is why I chose the place of execution.'

'I know,' she said impatiently. 'Before the residence of the Lady Moira.' Her eyes widened. 'Whose house is next to the Halatian Embassy!'

Dyne made no answer, his face bland, his eyes enigmatic, but Seena was no fool. She had lived too long in the hothouse atmosphere of court intrigue not to be able to see the obvious. Kund was wealthy, Halat was not. Many thought that the Lady Moira had a better claim to the throne than the Matriarch. Gloria was old.

'But to assassinate her?'

'You misunderstand, my lady,' said Dyne in his soft modulation. 'The assassination was not aimed at the Matriarch. It was aimed at yourself.'

★ ★ ★

A bell chimed from an inner room of the complex of inflated plastic which was their temporary home. A curtain swept aside and Gloria, the Matriarch of Kund, stood in the opening. She was very old but as a tree is old, grown tough with age and battle, hard and determined and drawing strength from that determination. Two of her guards attended her — hard-faced, mannish women, dedicated and fanatically loyal. She waved them aside as she moved towards a chair.

'I can manage. I'm not so old that you have to carry me about!'

Her voice, she knew, was too thin, too querulous but it was something that couldn't be helped. Not even the cosmosurgeons could revitalize delicate tissue which had aged too much. But it was a fault which, normally, she managed to control.

'All right,' she snapped at the guards as she sat down. 'Wait outside — out of earshot.' She waited until the curtain had fallen behind them. They would not go far, perhaps not far enough, but she could trust their discretion. She looked at Dyne.

'Well, did you tell her?'

'Yes, my lady.'

'And she was scared?' She chuckled as the cyber made no answer. 'She was scared. So was I the first time I realized that someone wanted to kill me. That was a long time ago now. A long time ago.' She was repeating herself, she realized; another attribute of age. Irritation made her cough.

'My lady!' Seena swept towards her, hovering at her side. 'Can I get you something? A drink? Anything?'

'Relax, girl, and don't fuss.' Gloria swallowed, easing her throat. 'You can't run away from unpleasant facts by forcing yourself to be busy with trifles. It's time you grew up and faced reality. Someone wanted you dead. Can you guess why?'

'No, my lady.'

'You can't even venture a guess?'

'Not that, my lady — I don't believe that anyone would want to assassinate me at all.'

'Then you're a fool!' Irritation made the old woman sharp. 'Take my word for it that they did. Now can you guess as to why?'

'Yes, my lady.' Her eyes very direct. 'To eliminate me from the possibility of succession.'

'Good!' Gloria smiled her pleasure. 'You're not as stupid as I hope some people think. Now you can get me the pomander.'

She sat back, relaxing in the chair as she sniffed the ball of golden filigree stuffed with exotic spices. She had always loved the scent of spice but the pomander held more than that. Liberated by the warmth of her hand microscopic particles of chemical magic rose from the ball to be absorbed by the mucous membranes of nose and mouth. Beneath their influence her body grew fractionally young again. Later she would pay for the demands made on her metabolism. Now it was important that she should not appear a senile old woman with a fogged and aimless mind.

'Tell me,' she said gently. 'What made you think that you could be considered as my heiress?'

'I don't think it,' said the girl. 'You asked me to give you a reason why I should be killed. I gave you one — but I don't believe that I was the target of the assassin.'

'You were,' snapped the old woman. 'Later you shall see the proof. Someone, somehow, guessed something they shouldn't and took steps to eliminate what they must have considered to be an obstruction. I would like to have those responsible in my power.' Her voice deepened, reflecting something of the cruelty of which she was capable.

'Do you know why you are a possible choice?'

Seena nodded, her face pale.

'Do you know what it means to be chosen?'

'Yes, my lady, I do.'

'I wonder.' Gloria looked at her ward with probing eyes. She was a beautiful, female animal. Perhaps too beautiful — but she would not have had her otherwise. 'Listen, girl,' she snapped, 'and understand. A Matriarch cannot be a slave to the emotional stress stemming from her reproductive organs. There is a cure — but it means the end of natural succession. A Matriarch can never be a mother. You see the problem?'

'Yes, my lady. Without a natural heir you have to choose your successor. In this you have advice.' Seena gestured towards Dyne. 'It is a matter of selecting the one best to rule.'

How simple the girl made it seem! The scent from the spice filled the room as the old woman lifted the pomander to her nostrils. This was no time for impatient anger.

'Best — for whom? For the great houses that wait like hungry dogs ready to snap up a bone? For the masses who have nothing but faith? For the cabals who seek power?' She shook her head. 'The one who takes my place must not be the tool of any such group. She must be without affiliation and misplaced loyalty. Above all she must be strong enough to hold the throne.'

'And,' reminded Dyne softly, 'she must be able to live long enough to collect it.'

'Right!' Gloria leaned forward in her chair, her eyes burning at her ward. 'Ten times in the past seven years I have seemed to favour a successor. Ten times has an assassin struck.' Her lips writhed

26

in sardonic amusement. 'I found it a convenient way of disposing of the over-ambitious.' She read the girl's expression. 'You don't like it? You think that any woman can rule with lily-white hands? Girl, I've held the throne for eighty years and it didn't come as a gift. I've fought for it every minute, pitting one house against another, letting them weaken themselves when to allow them to unite would have meant the end of my rule. I've killed and manoeuvred and done things no woman should ever have to do. But Kund is more important than any woman. Remember that!'

She was talking, thought Seena, as if to the next Matriarch.

* * *

The face was a mask of pain, the eyes enormous, the mouth a lipless hole of silent pain. Sweat ran down the deep-graven lines in the tormented face. Almost she could smell the rank odour from the masculine body.

'He was conditioned,' said Dyne

quietly at her side, 'in order to overcome the instilled death-directive we had to bypass the nervous system to the heart.' His arm was a shadow against the screen, his finger tapping softly on the glass as he pointed to where thick tubes ran from the chest to a squat machine. 'The conflict caused a revival of the birth-trauma. He wants to die and cannot and so feels psychological pain.'

'Must I watch this?'

'It is the Matriarch's order.' He did not look at her. In the light from the screen his face was a kaleidoscope of colour. 'It is important that you understand that you were the target of this assassin.'

'Why?'

'That, my lady, is not for me to say.' He stepped back as the scene diminished, showing the interior of the interrogation laboratory of the palace. 'I predicted that there was an eighty-two per cent probability of such an attempt being made. Watch was kept as I advised and the man was captured. His story was obviously false. Warned of what to expect the guards prevented his self-murder. Precautions were taken before his interrogation. He admitted that you were his target.'

'I don't believe it!' She was shaken by the sight, by the reminder of what went on behind the outwardly innocent façade of rule. 'Is this some kind of trick?'

'For what purpose, my lady?' He waited courteously for her reply and, when none came, reached out and touched a control. The scene blurred, expanded to show the tormented face, the lipless, gaping mouth. This time there was sound, a horrible rasp of breath, a whimpering threnody, a name. Her name.

'Enough!'

The face diminished, the sound died, the screen went blank. A curtain rustled and light poured into the room. Dyne turned from the window.

'It proved impossible to elicit the name of his employer and it is doubtful if he even knew it. There are ways to arrange these things. But I advised steps to be taken so that those probably responsible would know of their failure — and our knowledge of their implication.'

'By impaling him!'

'Yes, my lady.'

She shuddered, remembering the tormented face turned towards the sky, the ugly stains on the polished glass, the empty gropings of the hands, the aimless movements of the feet. And the screams — she could not easily forget the screams.

But she no longer blamed the Matriarch.

The room oppressed her with its too-recent memory of pain. A bare, bleak chamber used by the guards in attendance, empty now but for the cyber and herself. Impulsively she walked across the floor, through hangings of shimmering crystal, through an annex piled deep with rugs and to a narrow door opening on the world outside. She pressed the release and the panel folded to one side, letting in the tropic heat. She stood feeling the glare of the sun on her face, looking out to where the heavy waves of the ocean rolled sluggishly towards the shore. Some men in a crude boat fought the swell.

A rustle and Dyne was beside her. She pointed to the men, tiny in the distance.

'What are they doing?'

'Seeking food, my lady.'

She nodded, uninterested in the problems of others, her mind stained with thoughts of danger and death. Someone had tried to kill her — it was not a comforting thought.

'Why are we here?' She gestured towards the outside world. 'Why the sudden journey from Kund, the trans-shipping, the charter?'

'You were considered to be in grave danger, my lady. And the engines of our ship were not safe.'

'Sabotage?'

'It is possible.'

She felt a chill run down her spine. The great houses had wealth and power and their influence could reach far. In the struggle for the succession who could consider themselves safe? Impatiently she shook her head.

'Even so, why are we here? What does the Matriarch hope to find?'

'Perhaps an answer, my lady.' He paused, looking at her, recognizing her beauty as a mathematician would recognize the beauty of an abstract equation. In her, art and science had united with the original germ plasm to produce something exceptional. 'You know of Gath?'

'I have heard of it. This is the planet on which you are supposed to be able to hear the music of the spheres.' Her laugh was brittle, humourless. 'Did we come here to listen to music? If so we have wasted our journey. There are more pleasing sounds on Kund.'

'We are not in the right place, my lady. And this is not the right time. We must wait for the storm.'

'And?'

'Prior to the storm we will go north, to a place where the coast swings east towards the cold and dark of the night hemisphere. There stands a tremendous barrier, a mountain range fretted and carved by endless winds, worn by the passage of time. Hard stone remains while soft has been weathered away. Buried deep in the rock are masses of crystal which respond in a wide range of harmonics to pressure and vibration. In effect the range is the greatest sounding board ever imagined. When the winds blow during a storm the results are — interesting.'

'You have been here before?'

'No, my lady.'

'Then — ?' She broken off the question, knowing the answer. Given a pair of facts Dyne could find a third. Given a set of circumstances and the cyber could extrapolate the most probable course of events. It was enough for him to know what had been experienced by others. But still a question remained.

'Why?'

'Why are we here? What is there about Gath which drew the Matriarch all the way from Kund?' He made no pretence that he didn't grasp her meaning. 'I told you, my lady. It could be that she hopes to find an answer.'

3

The boat was crude, rough planks lashed
with scraps of wire, plastic, plaited vines.
It had no sail, no keel, only thwarts for
the rowers, a rudder, a pointed prow. An
outrigger had been added as an after-
thought but even so the vessel was as
seaworthy as a coracle.

'Row!'

The skipper, bare feet hard on the
bottom, bare chest reflecting the sun,
yelled the order. His voice was bigger
than it should be. Too big when
compared with the stark cage of his ribs,
the skeletal planes of his face.

'Row, damn you!' he yelled. 'Row!'

Dumarest grunted as he threw his
weight on his oar. Like the boat itself it
was crudely fashioned by men who had
scant knowledge and less skill. A boat, to
them, was something which floated. They
knew nothing of balance, correct ratios,
the art which turned dead wood into a

thing alive. They had simply built a platform from which to raid the sea.

He grunted again as he tugged at the stubborn pole with the flattened end. Water oozed from between the planks and wet his bare feet. The sun was hot on his naked back. He had won his place because he was big, because he seemed fit, because he could swim. Megan was guarding his clothes.

'There!' The skipper pointed and leaned his weight against the rudder. Something had broken the surface and he headed towards it. 'Faster!' he yelled. 'Faster!'

They did their best. None of them was strong, strength needs food. None of them were fat, travellers were never that. All were desperate — starvation was all too real a threat. So they flung their weight at the oars, gasping in the heat, fevered in their hunting frenzy.

The skipper tensed as they drew close to the spot he had marked. He would get two shares of whatever they caught. Three would go to the owner of the boat safe on shore. The rest would get one share each.

'Steady!' He eased the rudder and dashed sweat from his eyes. He was over-anxious and knew it but it had been too long since he made a catch. Small fish, sure, with half of them going back for bait. Skinny, fleshless things of little nutritional value, costing more strength to get than they gave. But whatever had broken the surface had been big. 'Carl!' he ordered. 'Get set!'

A tall, thin, caricature of a man nodded, dropped his oar, took up his place in the prow. He hefted a harpoon attached to a coil of rope. He looked over his shoulder at the skipper.

'All set, Abe.'

'Watch it!' Abe squinted against the sun. The leaden surface of the sea broke, rolled, something hard and grey flashing in the ruby light. 'There, Carl! There!'

The harpoon darted forward, the barbs biting deep. Immediately Carl dived for his oar. Dumarest knocked him aside.

'The rope, man! Watch the rope!'

'Get out of my way!' Carl clawed for his oar as the rope ran out. The boat jerked, began to move. Desperately the skipper yelled orders.

'Back! Back for your lives!'

The water threshed as the crude oars lashed the swell. It was like trying to halt the movement of a glacier. The rope thrummed as the prow began to tilt forward. Water streamed over the gunwale.

'The rope!' Dumarest reached out, snatched a knife from the belt of the harpooner, dragged the edge across the fibre. It parted, the short end lashing back, the prow rising. Beneath them something moved, broke the surface beyond the stern.

'You fool!' Carl snatched back the knife. 'You've lost us the rope.'

'Better that than our lives.' Dumarest looked at the skipper. 'Is this how you go fishing?'

'Do you know of a better way?' He was on safe ground. He had fished this sea before, Dumarest hadn't. 'Without nets how else do you think we can catch the big ones? We stick them, tire them, drag them to shore. Without a rope how can we do that?'

His anger was justified. The fish had

been big, perhaps three days eating for them all and with some left over. He opened his mouth to vent more of his rage then closed it as a man yelled.

'Look, Abe. Blood!'

A thin red film darkened the surface. A thin something trailed across it and Carl shouted his recognition.

'The rope!'

He dived before anyone could stop him. He plunged smoothly beneath the waves, rose swimming, headed towards the thin strand of the rope. He grabbed it, turned, began to swim back to the boat. He reached it, clawed at the gunwale, began to heave himself aboard. He couldn't make it and clung gasping to the rough wood.

'Help him.' Abe searched the sea with anxious eyes. 'Hurry!'

Dumarest reached the clinging man, clamped his hands around Carl's upper arms, adjusted his weight for the upwards pull.

'Thanks,' said Carl. 'I guess — ' He broke off, a peculiar expression on his face. It lasted for about three seconds, then he began to scream.

Dumarest realized why when he dragged the man into the boat. Both his legs had been severed above the knees.

* * *

The wakening was strange. There was a booming rhythm with a repetitive beat and a liquid, sucking gurgle that he had never heard before. The eddy currents seemed to be working for he could feel heat on his body but his mouth was filled with an alien taste and the gritty sensation beneath his body was something outside of his experience. But the light was the same — too bright. The light was always too bright.

He rolled and was immediately awake. He wasn't in a box. He wasn't in a ship which had just ended its passage. He lay on a beach of gritty sand with the sun a ruby glare over the water which rolled and thundered on the sloping shore.

He rolled again so that he was face downwards and rose to all fours. Immediately he was violently sick. He backed like a dog from a suspicious odour and felt wetness beneath his hand. It was a pool of water left by the receding tide and he washed his face and mouth in the saline liquid. Only when he had swallowed a little did he realize that he burned with thirst.

The booming of the surf did nothing to relieve his craving for water.

He rose to his knees and fought a wave of giddiness. His weakness was terrifying. He sat down staring out to sea, waiting for the giddiness to pass. He was naked but for his shorts — somehow he had lost his trousers and belt. His skin was caked with salt and something had removed a strip of skin down the side of one thigh. He pressed the wound. Blood oozed from the place which looked as if it had been flayed.

After a long while he rose to his feet and turned to stare at the shore.

The beach was narrow, a strip of sand caught in the arc of a bay ending at high walls of eroded stone. Boulders lay at the foot, a green slime reaching to well above his head, while trapped pools of water reflected the sunlight as if pools of blood. To either side the surf pounded against the jutting sides of the bay.

He was sick again before he reached the cliff, his stomach emptying itself of swallowed salt. He paused to rinse his mouth at one of the pools, resisted the temptation to slake his thirst with the saline poison, then stared at what he must climb.

For a fit man it would have been difficult, for a traveller it would always have been hard, in his present condition it was almost impossible. Yet he had no choice. He had to climb or drown. He looked at the sea. He had lain longer than he suspected, already the waves were lapping higher. Stepping back he surveyed the cliff, chose his route and began to climb.

He reached a height of twelve feet then his hand slipped on green slime and he fell. He tried again, this time further along the cliff, but fell almost at once. The third time he was almost stunned, lying and wondering if he had broken a bone. He hadn't. The next time he tried he knew it was his last attempt.

He was sweating as he passed the level of the slime, his heart pounding as if it would burst from his chest. He clung to the rock, wishing that he had his boots, driving the tender flesh of his toes against the unyielding stone. He crawled higher and found a long, slanting crack that had been invisible from below. It carried him to within ten feet of the edge before it petered out. He craned his head, trying to see beyond the overhang, trying to ignore the cramped agony in hands and feet. Vegetation had overgrown the edge, tendrils of it hanging low but too thin to offer assistance. A gnarled root caught his eye.

It was too far to reach, a foot beyond the tips of his fingers and awkwardly placed. He gauged the distance and jumped without hesitation. His right hand missed, his left caught and he hung suspended by one hand. The root gave beneath the strain. He twisted, clawing upwards with his right hand and felt it hit a snag of hidden rock. He heaved, scrabbling with his feet. He grabbed upwards with his left hand, rested a foot against the root, thrust himself desperately upwards. A trail of dirt fell to the beach as he rested his elbows on the edge. One final effort and he was out of danger.

He'd walked twenty feet before he realized it and then his legs simply collapsed. He fell to the ground, sobbing for breath, his body a mass of pain.

And, after a long while, Megan found him.

* * *

'I saw what happened,' he said. He sat beside a small fire, a can over the flames, an appetizing smell coming from the can. 'At least I saw the boat capsize and all of you flung into the sea. I don't know the details.'

Dumarest told him. Megan nodded, busy over his fire. Carefully he fed a handful of dried grass into the flames. Smoke rose about the can and plumed into the sky.

'The blood would have attracted the big ones,' he said. 'Maybe the one you'd harpooned. They come in close to shore quite a bit, especially before a storm.' He dipped a spoon into the can, tasted it, added more fuel to the fire. 'From what I could see it was a real mess. You were lucky to escape.'

The luck had been incredible. Dumarest remembered a time of confusion with the skipper yelling orders. There had been a scrabble of men trying to reach the oars. Carl's screams had faded as the carmine fountain carried away his life. Then something had risen from beneath, smashing the boat, overturning it as the outrigger collapsed.

Then had come the water, the struggle and stomach-knotting fear, the final state of near-unconsciousness when he had lain on his back and floated and concentrated on the single necessity of breath.

'I thought you might be washed ashore,' said Megan. He didn't look at the big man. 'I bought a few things and came looking. I used your money.'

He could have stolen it with far less effort.

'Here.' Megan lifted the can from the

fire. 'Get this down while it's still hot.'

It was good food, expensive, probably bought from the Resident's store. Dumarest spooned it down, savouring every drop. When the can was two-thirds empty he handed it to Megan.

'Finish it.'

'No, Earl. You need it more than I do.'

'Finish it and don't be a fool. I'm not strong enough to carry you back to camp. Now eat up and let's get moving.'

Megan had brought more than food. He knew what could happen to men cast into the sea. Dumarest dressed while the other ate, then packed and finally stamped out the fire. Together they set off across a rolling plain covered with stunted vegetation. The ground was uneven, treacherous with gnarled roots and half-buried stones. They walked slowly, taking care where they set their feet.

'We're about half-way between the camp and the mountains,' said Megan. 'We should hit the path soon. The going will be easier then.'

Dumarest nodded, making no comment. Megan had followed the coast every foot of the way from the camp. It had been a long, hard trip. He slowed his pace a little. 'This vegetation should provide food and cover for game,' he said thoughtfully as the other drew level. 'Are you sure there isn't any?'

Megan shook his head. 'Not that I know of. I suppose there could be something small but I've never seen any.' He stumbled and almost fell. 'Damn it,' he swore. 'Where's that path?'

They reached it two hours later. It was broad, smooth, lined with boulders which had obviously been rolled aside to permit an easy passage. The ground was springy underfoot, the grass showing signs of recent growth. Megan halted and pointed towards the north.

'The mountains are up there,' he said. 'You might just be able to see them.'

Dumarest climbed a boulder, narrowed his eyes and saw a distant hump against the purple sky. He looked higher and saw the pale crescent of a moon. A second showed against the pale stars far to the east. He turned and the sun, low on the horizon, burned into his eyes. Sun, moons and stars mingled in this strange region of the twilight zone. He stood for a long while studying the scene. A painter would have envied him. Gath was a strange planet. He said so and Megan shrugged.

'It's a ghost world,' he said as Dumarest rejoined him. 'There's a place up near those mountains where the dead rise to walk again.'

Dumarest looked at him. The man was serious.

'I'd heard about it,' said Megan. 'When I landed I wanted to investigate. I did. Now I wish to hell that I hadn't.'

'Sounds,' said Dumarest. 'Noises. A trick of acoustics. Since when have you been scared of an echo?'

'It's more than that.' Megan was no longer dirty but even the chemical concentrates Dumarest had bought required time to build tissue. His eyes were brooding shadows in the hollows of his face. 'Maybe you'll find that out for yourself.'

'Now?'

'Not until the storm. The conditions aren't right until then. When they are — you hear things.'

'Celestial music?' Dumarest smiled. 'That's what the admen say.'

'For once they tell the truth,' said Megan shortly. He started down the path away from the mountains.

4

A ship landed as they returned to camp. From it stepped a group of tourists, gay, laughing, an assorted batch. The entourage of the Prince of Emmened who had ruined a world by his whims and would ruin more unless stopped by an assassin. Three cowled monks of the Universal Brotherhood, two musicians, an artist, four poets, an entrepeneur. All had travelled High, some were still slow in movement, slower in speech from the lingering effects of quick-time.

Three had travelled Low; a man, little more than a boy, a withered crone stronger than she looked, a fool.

He came staggering from the ship bowed beneath the weight of a fibroid box as large as himself. He was grotesquely thin. His eyes burned like coals from the gaunt pallor of his face. Ribs showed prominent against the flesh of his chest bare beneath the ragged shirt. He was a shambling scarecrow of a man.

'Gath!' He cried out and fell to the seared dirt of the field, pressing his cheek against the soil. The box which he carried by means of a strap over his shoulders gave him the appearance of a monstrous beetle. 'Gath!'

His companions ignored him. The tourists looked and saw nothing of interest. All travellers were mad. The handler stood at the door of his ship and spat after his late charges.

'Gath!' yelled the man again. He tried to rise but the weight of the box pressed him to the ground. Eel-like he wriggled from beneath, slipping the strap from his shoulders, kneeling by the box. He patted it, crooning inarticulate sounds. Saliva dribbled from his mouth and wet his chin.

'Mad,' said Megan positively. 'Insane.'

'In trouble.' Dumarest was interested. Megan shrugged.

'So he's in trouble. So are we. Let's go and see if we can earn something by making ourselves useful to the tourists.'

'You go.' Dumarest strode towards the

kneeling man. Megan scowled, then followed. Dumarest halted beside the crooning man.

'You need help,' he said flatly. 'Do you want us to help you?'

'Help?' The man looked up. His eyes were yellowish, muddy. 'Is this Gath?'

Dumarest nodded.

'Then everything's all right.' He rose and clutched Dumarest by the arm. 'Tell me, is it true what they say about this place?'

'The voices?' Megan nodded. 'It's true.'

'Thank God!' Abruptly the man grew calm. Slowly he wiped the saliva from his mouth with the cuff of his sleeve. 'I — I never thought I'd get here.' He swallowed. 'My name is Sime. I've very little money but if you will help me I'll — '

'We ask no pay.' Dumarest nodded to Megan and together they stooped over the box. It was over six feet long and shaped like a coffin. Megan grunted as he felt the weight.

'What's in here? Lead?'

'Just some things,' said Sime. He looked anxious. 'Just carry it from the field. I'll be able to manage it after I rest for a while. Just carry it from the field.'

Slowly they moved towards the camp. Megan stumbled, swore as his ankle turned, sprang clear as his end of the box fell with a thud. The vibration tore the box from Dumarest's hands. The lid, jarred by the fall, began to swing open.

'Careful!' Sime flung himself on the lid. His hands trembled as he secured the fastenings. 'You'll hurt — ' He caught himself. 'Please be careful.'

He hovered to one side as they carried the box into camp. Both men were sweating as they eased down their burden. A handful of travellers looked on with dull curiosity. Megan, straightening his back, glared at one who laughed.

'Something funny?'

'I think so.' The old crone who had travelled with Sime cackled all the louder. 'Why be so careful, dearies? You can't hurt what's in there.'

'Shut your mouth!' Sime stepped forward. 'You hear me? Now you just shut your mouth!'

'Try and shut it for me!' She cackled at

the thin man. 'Maybe they'd like to hear it.'

'Tell us, mother,' urged Megan. Immediately she flew into a rage.

'Don't you call me that! Do it again and I'll stab out your eyes!'

Megan recoiled from the long needle in her hand. 'No offence, my lady, but why did you say what you did?'

'About this?' She kicked the box. 'About this coffin?' She leered at Sime. 'He's got his dead wife in there, dearie. You can't hurt the dead.'

* * *

The monks had set up their church in the camp leaving Brother Angelo in charge. He sat in the close confines of the booth feeling the turgid heat from outside penetrate his rough, homespun habit, prickling his skin with a thousand tiny discomforts. He dismissed them as of no importance thinking instead of the never-ending task of his order, the continual striving to turn men from what they were into what they should be.

He was, he realized, verging into the sin of pride and jerked himself back to the immediate present. Through the mesh he could see a pale face, wide-eyed, trembling with released emotion. The litany of sin was all too-familiar, the human animal is capable only of certain emotions, certain acts which dull by constant repetition. But sin was too heavy a burden for any man to carry.

'. . . and, Brother, one time I stole a ration of food. I went to the pot twice and lied when questioned. It was fish stew. I ate what should have gone to another — but I was so hungry.'

Hunger of the spirit more than that of the body — yet could a man be blamed for wanting to survive? Brother Angelo considered the question as the list of petty sins grew. If man was animal, as he basically was, then survival was all-important and yet if he was more than animal, which he undoubtedly was, then he should not yield to his base appetites.

And yet, if he died because of consideration to his higher self, what then?

Such thoughts verged on heresy and Brother Angelo recognized the insidious attraction of theological disputation. It was not for him to question — only for him to act. If he could ease the burden of one man then his life would not have been in vain. The Universal teaching of complete Brotherhood held the answer to all pain, all hurt, all despair. No man is an island. All belong to the *corpus humanite*. The pain of one is the pain of all. And if all men could but recognize the truth of the credo — *there, but for the grace of God, go I* — the millenium would have arrived.

He would never see it. Men bred too fast, travelled too far for that. But it was something for which to live. A purpose for his dedication.

The thin voice from beyond the mesh ceased its litany of sin. The pale face was tense, the eyes hungry with anticipation. Brother Angelo switched on the benediction light. In the swirling kaleidoscope of colours the face seemed less animal, more ethereal.

'Look into the light of forgiveness,' he

said softly. 'Bathe in the flame of righteousness and be cleansed of all pain, all sin. Yield to the benediction of the Universal Brotherhood.'

The light was hypnotic, the subject subservient, the monk a trained master of his craft. The pale face relaxed, the eyes lost their hunger, peace smoothed the features. Subjectively the man was undergoing stringent penance. Later he would receive the bread of forgiveness.

Brother Benedict looked back as he reached the rise on which stood Hightown. He could see the pennant of the church and could imagine the file of men waiting to enter the booth. A younger monk would have been pleased at the display of religious fervour; Brother Benedict knew that the majority of them wanted only the wafer of concentrates which followed the communion.

Yet first they had to pass beneath the benediction-light. It was a fair exchange.

The streets of Hightown were wide, well-paved, free of dust and dirt. His sandals made little scraping noises as he trod the crushed stone surrounding the prefabricated hutments. A tourist, supine in a figure-chair, lifted a lazy hand in greeting.

'Welcome, Brother. Have you come to convert the heathen?'

'I come so that men may have the opportunity of indulging in the virtue of charity.' Brother Benedict held out his symbolical begging bowl. It was of cheap plastic, chipped, scarred, as rough as his habit. 'Of your charity, sir.'

'Why?' The tourist was willing to be amused. 'Why should I throw away what I have?'

'Men are starving within sight. Is that not reason enough?'

It wasn't and he knew it but he had played this game so often that he knew the expected responses by heart. His habit would command a certain amused indulgence. His request would stimulate jaded wits. His arguments were the prelude to reluctant disbursal. The trick was in making the hearer want to give. Therefore he must never be made to feel inferior, mean or small.

'Men are cheap,' pointed out the

tourist. 'Tell me, Brother, it is just that the weak should live at the expense of the strong?'

'No, brother, it is not,' agreed Benedict. His eyes were sharp as they examined the man. Smooth, rosily fat, dressed in luxurious fabrics. A glint of bright metal shone from a finger. A ring, curiously engraved, flashed in the sun. Benedict recognized the symbol. 'You play, brother?'

'Gamble?' The tourist looked startled. Many had so looked before Benedict's direct gaze. They didn't realize how they betrayed themselves. 'How did you know — ? Yes, I gamble.'

'And therefore you believe in luck.' The monk nodded. 'Life is a lottery, my friend. We are born — in circumstances over which we have no control. Some inherit wealth, others poverty. Some have the gift of intelligence and the power of command. Others have nothing and die with what they were born. In the game of life not all can win.'

'True.' The tourist looked thoughtful. His expression deepened as Benedict continued.

'At the tables, when you win, do you not toss a chip to the croupier? Do you not spend a little so as to assuage the lady you worship? The Lady Luck.'

'You know gamblers, brother.'

'Then, in this game of life in which you have been so fortunate, why not toss a little to those who have nothing?' Benedict extended his bowl. 'To the losers, brother, to those who are born to fail.'

He felt no pride as the tourist threw money into the bowl. The man had been generous but pride was a sin. And a beggar had no cause to be proud.

★ ★ ★

Piers Quentin, Resident Factor of Gath, moodily rubbed his pattern-shaved face and stared at the bloodshot orb of the sun. Slowly it was sinking towards the leaden waves of the ocean. Irritably he wished that it would hurry up.

It was always the same before a storm, this feeling he had of mounting tension and growing irritation. Bad traits for a man who had to soothe the rich and powerful. Worse when he had to tread the narrow path between ensuring their comfort and safety and risking their displeasure. Yet each time the storm came due and the ships began to arrive he felt the same. As if each storm was a crisis which had to be met and surmounted. As if one day the crisis would prove too great. He didn't like to think of what could happen then.

'You are troubled, brother.' Brother Ely, old and shrewd in the ways of men, looked at the resident's rigid back from where he sat at ease in a padded chair. A cool drink stood by his hand, ice tinkling in the limpid depths. The resident, while not religious, was not ungenerous. 'Is it the storm?'

'It's always the storm.' Piers turned from the window and began to pace the floor. 'Out there,' he gestured towards Hightown, 'is probably the greatest assembly of wealth and power to be found in the uninhabited worlds. Traditional enemies, entrepreneurs, place-seekers and time-servers, opportunists and the rest, all crammed cheek to jowl, all waiting

— all spoiling for trouble.'

'Surely you exaggerate?' Ely picked up his drink and sipped the contents. His mouth constricted to the tart flavour of lime. 'Are things so bad?'

'Worse.' Piers halted beside the dispenser and poured himself a drink. It was almost pure alcohol. He swallowed it at a single gulp. 'These storms are something special, brother. Already the solar flare has closed the space lines. Above the atmosphere is a hell of naked radiation which would penetrate the strongest shield carried by a commercial vessel. That is why the ships arrive early. That is why the tension is so high.'

'I hadn't noticed,' said Ely. 'But then, I lack your experience.'

'You'll sense it soon enough,' promised the resident. 'The air is full of stray ions, heavy with undischarged electrical potential. Nerves are overtense. Tempers are too thin. The Devil is loose among us.' He helped himself to another drink. 'Trouble,' he mourned. 'I stand on the brink of a volcano. A touch is enough to destroy me.'

The monk said nothing. He had come to pay his respects; he had stayed to listen to the outpourings of a tormented soul.

'The satellites are moving into position,' continued the resident. 'Soon their juxtaposition will affect the stability of Gath and then — '

'The storm?'

'The storm.' Piers swallowed his drink, poured another. He felt the impact of the monk's eyes, recognized their displeasure, irritably set down the glass. 'By that time everyone will be north, standing before the mountain. God knows what may happen then — I can only guess. It is time for you to pray, brother.'

'Always it is time to pray,' corrected the monk gravely. 'The psychological effect of channelled thought cannot be overestimated.' He hesitated. 'Neither can adherence to the Supreme Ethic.'

'I am not my brother's keeper,' snapped Piers sharply. He took up his drink, looked at it, gulped it down. 'You're thinking of Lowtown, of course.'

'The camp? Yes.'

'I didn't ask them to come here.

Penniless travellers swept up by the vagaries of space. Do you think I want them around?'

He strode to the window, looked through it, stared towards the camp. He had never minimized the danger of starving men, the strength of desperation. On this planet wealth and poverty were too close. They had nothing but a little distance between them. One day, perhaps during a storm, that distance wouldn't be enough. Even now a strong man could . . . He shuddered at the prospect.

'They are a part of humanity,' said Ely gently. He was accustomed to the sight of poverty. 'Remember, brother, there, but for the grace of God, go you.'

'Spare me the sermon, monk.'

'Not a sermon, brother. Facts. They are here. You are the resident. They are your responsibility.'

'No!' Piers was emphatic. 'I refuse to accept your moral judgement. In law they are nothing. They came here by their own free will. They can leave the same way or stay until they rot. I am not responsible.' Irritably he again paced the floor. He hesitated by the dispenser then moved away. He refused to meet Ely's eyes. 'I do what I can,' he protested. 'Each storm I arrange for a passage and run a lottery. The winner gets the passage. Sometimes, if the money is enough, more can win the prize.'

'Money?' Ely raised his eyebrows. 'Here?'

'They can earn a little from the visitors.' Piers didn't want to go into details. 'Between storms I employ them at various tasks. I pay them in chemical concentrates.'

'Charity, brother?'

Piers didn't miss the irony. 'I do what I can,' he insisted stubbornly. 'I can do no more.'

Brother Ely made no comment. He'd had long practice in hiding emotion; almost as long to learn how to read it. The resident would end a very rich man. But he was an unhappy one. The ice in his glass rattled as he held it to the spout of the dispenser. He had much about which to feel guilt.

'Damn it, brother,' he said plaintively. 'I do my best.'

64

* ★ *

Ely met Dyne as he left the Resident's quarters. The monk stiffened as he saw the cyber. Both felt the reaction of strange cats to each other. The Universal Brotherhood had no trust for the Cyclan. The cybers had no love for the monks.

They looked at each other, Dyne in his rich scarlet, Ely in his drab homespun. One could feel no emotion, the other dealt with little else.

'A fine day, brother,' said Ely gently. The silence once broken, Dyne could not ignore the monk. It would be illogical to arouse irritation. Cybers made no enemies and tried to make everyone their friend.

'It is always day on Gath,' he said in his soft modulation; the trained voice which contained no irritant factors. 'You have just arrived?'

'On the last ship to reach this world before the storm.' Ely sensed the other's dislike as a dog would scent anger or fear. 'You are alone?'

'I serve the Matriarch of Kund.'

65

'Naturally.' Ely stepped to one side. 'I must not detain you, brother. Go in peace.'

Dyne bowed, a slight, almost imperceptible inclination of his head, then swept on his way. Two of his retinue guarded his private quarters, young, sternly moulded men, novitiates to the Cyclan, officially his personal attendants.

'Total seal,' ordered Dyne. Even command did not harden his voice. There was no need of aural emphasis. 'No interruption of any kind for any reason.'

Inside his quarters he rested supine on a narrow couch. Touching the bracelet locked about his left wrist he stepped up the power. The device ensured that no one could ever spy on a cyber, no scanner or electronic ear could focus in his vicinity. It was a precaution, nothing more.

Relaxing he closed his eyes and concentrated on the Samatchazi formulae. Gradually he lost the senses of taste, smell, touch and hearing. Had he opened his eyes he would have been blind. Locked in the womb of his skull his brain ceased to be irritated by external stimuli. It became a thing of pure intellect, its reasoning awareness its only thread with life. Only then did the grafted Homochon elements become active. Rapport soon followed.

Dyne became really alive.

Each cyber had a different experience. For him it was as if every door in the universe had opened to let in the shining light of truth. He was a living part of an organism which stretched across space in countless crystalline droplets, each glowing with intelligence. Filaments connected one to the other so that it was as if he saw a dew-scattered web stretching to infinity. Saw it and was a part of it; was it while it was himself, sharing yet owning the tremendous gestalt of minds.

At the centre of the web was the headquarters of the Cyclan. Buried beneath miles of rock, deep in the heart of a lonely planet, the central intelligence absorbed his knowledge as a sponge would suck the water from a pond. There was no verbal communication; only mental communion in the form of words,

quick, almost instantaneous, organic trans-
mission against which even supra-radio
was the merest crawl.

'*Verification received of anticipated
development of situation on Gath.
Continue as directed.*'

That was all.

The rest was sheer mental intoxication.

There was always this period after
rapport during which the Homochon
elements sank back into quiescence and
the machinery of the body began to
re-align itself with mental control. Dyne
floated in a black nothingness while he
sensed strange memories and unlived
situations. Scraps of overflow from other
intelligences — the throw-away waste of
other minds. The power of central
intelligence of the tremendous cybernetic
complex which was the heart of the
Cyclan.

One day he would be a part of that
intelligence. His body would age and his
senses dull but his mind would remain as
active as ever. Then they would take him
and rid his intelligence of the hampering
flesh so that he could join the others,

hooked in series to the naked brains pulsing in their nutrient fluid, thousands and thousands of such brains all tuned to a common end.

Millions of such brains, perhaps. Millions of freed intelligence working to solve the problems of the universe.

A gestalt against which there could be no resistance.

5

Megan left the church, the taste of the wafer strong in his mouth, the euphoric drug with which it had been treated banishing his depression. It was always like this after he had been cleansed. He felt strong and fit and full of inner quietude. The mood would last for a time and then would begin to fade. Then, if the church was still around, he would go back for another wafer.

He found Dumarest sitting on a dune by the shore staring out to sea. He held a great bunch of grass in one hand and slowly pulled each stem between his teeth. After every dozen or so stems, he swallowed the collected pulp. Discarded grass lay in a mound between his feet. He lacked the digestive system which would have converted the cellulose into nourishment.

Megan squatted beside him. He found stones and idly tossed them into the water. Dumarest spat out a stem of grass.

'Well, are you cleansed, fed and of sound mind?'

'You shouldn't joke about the Brotherhood,' protested Megan. 'The monks do a lot of good work.' He felt the sudden need to share his contentment. 'Why don't you go along, Earl? The wafer's worth getting at least.'

'You think so?' Dumarest busied himself with more grass. 'I didn't know that you were religious.'

'I'm not.' Megan was quick to deny the accusation. 'Well, not really. I first went while I was on Lund. More for a joke than anything else.' He looked at Dumarest. 'No, that isn't true. I thought I needed some help. I wanted comforting. The monks gave me what I needed.'

'And you've been going to church ever since?'

'In a way. Nothing special, you understand, but if there's a church and I've got the time — ' Megan dug the toe of his boot into the sand. 'It doesn't do any harm.'

'No?'

'Well, does it?'

Dumarest didn't answer. He was thinking of the long walk along the coast, the spending of the last coin for the benefit of a man Megan had every reason to think dead. In him the Supreme Ethic had bitten deep. It amused Dumarest to realize that, in a way, he owed the Brotherhood his life. One day he might thank them.

He dragged more grass between his teeth and swallowed the tasteless pulp. His eyes were sombre as he stared out to sea. Out there, beneath the waves, was all the food a man could wish but he couldn't get it. The only boat was gone and none would sail with him if they could. He had gained the reputation of being bad luck.

It could be true. Maybe he had done wrong in cutting the rope but he didn't waste time thinking about it. He was not a man who regretted the past.

Not when the future looked so black.

Irritably he flung away the grass, conscious of the hunger clawing at his stomach. The pulp had done nothing but accentuate his appetite. Unless he got food soon he would begin the slide into malnutrition, actual starvation together with the weakness and killing apathy which made it hard to think, harder still to act.

Rising he looked down at Megan. 'I'm going to find something to eat,' he said. 'Want to come along?'

'The Brothers will feed you.' Megan sprang up, smiling as if he had solved the problem. 'They'll give you a wafer and maybe something later if they can beg it from Hightown.' He fell into step beside the big man. 'You going to try them, Earl?'

'No.'

'You got something against them?'

'Not if they've got food to give away — but I'm not going to church.'

'Then — ?' It was a question. The camp held no spare food. Everything had a price and food the highest of all. Dumarest had no money and nothing to sell other than his clothes. But he had his hands. Instinctively they clenched at Megan's question.

'I don't know yet,' he said sharply. 'I've

got to look around and see what's going. But if there's food to be had I'm going to get it. I'm not going to sit and starve while I've the strength to go looking.'

Or, thought Megan dully, the strength to take. He hurried ahead hoping to find one of the monks and enlist his support. Dumarest was in a dangerous mood and it could kill him. To rob Lowtown was to invite later reprisal. To risk Hightown was to beg the guards to shoot him dead for his effrontery. For his own sake he would have to be stopped.

Dumarest caught up with him as they reached the camp. The place was deserted. Even the central fire had lost its usual group toasting scraps of food over the flames. The pennant on the plastic church hung limply from its standard. The monks were not to be seen. Megan looked suddenly afraid.

'No,' he said. 'It's too soon. They couldn't have started for the mountains yet.' He was afraid of the loss of potential employment.

'They're up near the field,' said Dumarest. He stared at a cluster of distant figures. 'Let's go and see what's doing.'

★　★　★

The Prince of Emmened was bored and had taken steps to relieve his boredom. He sat at the edge of a cleared space towards the perimeter of the field, safe among his sycophants, venting his displeasure with a languid yawn.

'Why do they hesitate?' he complained. 'Moidor will stiffen.' He beamed at his favourite, standing, almost nude, in the centre of the cleared space. Muscles rippled beneath oiled skin marred only by the brand of Emmened high on one shoulder. He was a creature of the prince, a trained fighter of animals and men.

'They are weak, my lord.' A courtier leaned close to the prince's ear. 'These travellers are starved and of no real sport. It is a pity that the Matriarch did not accept our challenge.'

'One of her guards against Moidor?' Emmened pursed his lips with disappointment. It had seemed a good idea when Crowder had first mentioned it. It still seemed a good idea. A mixed-sex battle always held spice. 'Did she receive the suggestion?'

'She ignored it, my lord.' Crowder knew better than to relate the exact words in which Gloria had spurned the offer. 'It could be that she fears for the safety of her followers.'

Emmened nodded as he stared at his royal guest. The Matriarch had condescended to attend his diversion. She sat beneath an awning of brilliant yellow, her ward at her side, Dyne a scarlet shadow to her rear. Her guards ringed the party, staring cold-eyed at the crowd.

'Moidor has a reputation,' mused the prince. 'It could be that she was afraid of the outcome.' He leaned forward a little, eyes glowing as he studied the lithe figure of the girl. 'Her maid?'

'The Lady Thoth, my lord.'

'I have a thought,' whispered the prince. 'If you could arrange for me to have a private, personal match with her you would be the richer by the wealth of a city.'

'You have excellent taste, my lord. She is indeed a lovely woman.' Crowder took care not to look at the subject of their discussion. The woman-guards had keen eyes and were jealous of the honour of their charges. 'Stir her passion with the sight of blood and — who knows?'

Emmened smiled and Crowder felt a sudden chill. His prince was a creature of cruel whims and sadistic notions. Should he order the courtier to deliver the girl to his bed, and he should fail as fail he must, then it would be wiser for him to swallow poison.

'Raise the offer,' said Emmened abruptly. 'Tempt the fools to fight — and tell Moidor not to be gentle. We need the sight of blood.' He looked deliberately at the girl, his eyes hot with anticipation.

Dumarest followed the direction of his stare. He saw the old woman, the girl at her side. His face hardened as he recognized the scarlet robe of the cyber. Megan whispered at his side.

'That's the party which arrived with you.'

'I know.' Dumarest had nothing to

thank them for. He tightened his stomach against its emptiness. Sweat ran down his face. The heat was that of an oven.

Crowder came forward, walking the perimeter of the cleared space.

'A traveller's passage to any who can win a single fall,' he shouted. 'High travel to anyone who can kill.'

Dumarest swayed forward.

'Earl!' Megan clutched at his arm. 'Has that grass sent you crazy? You wouldn't stand a chance against an animal like that.'

Crowder had noticed the slight movement. He came closer, smiling, repeating the offer and adding a little more bait.

'A passage for a single fall. High travel if you kill. A hundred units if you try.' Coins shone hypnotically in his hand. His smile widened as Dumarest stepped forward. 'You?'

'Yes.'

'Do you want to strip, oil, prepare yourself?'

'No.' Dumarest was curt. 'Give me the money.'

'A moment. Would you prefer to fight

armed? Knives, perhaps?'

'As I am.' Dumarest held out his hand. 'Give me the money.' Crowder shrugged and passed over the coins. Dumarest threw them to Megan, rubbed his hands on the sides of his shirt, then stepped towards the fighter. Moidor smiled.

He was a beautiful animal and he knew it. He postured, flexing his muscles so that the sun gleamed on lumps and ridges of tissue, threw shadows into the hollows and concave places. He had spent his life developing his body. He looked indestructible.

'Come,' he smiled as Dumarest stepped forwards. 'Come into my arms, my brave one. Feel my embrace — and die!'

His voice was a little slurred, his smile and gesture a little slow. His eyes needed time to change focus. Quick-time still lingered in his blood and compressed the passing seconds. His reflexes were not operating at their normal speed but he was still dangerous. Dumarest didn't have to look at the two dead men to remind himself of that. But it gave him a thin chance whereas, if the fighter were normal, he would have no chance at all.

'You wait,' purred Moidor. 'You hesitate. Do not be afraid. I bring death as a friend.'

He stepped forward, smiling, his arms rising to shoulder height.

'Now,' he whispered.

Dumarest kicked him in the knee.

* * *

He lashed out with his full force, throwing his shoulders back from the reaching hands, pivoting on his hip. He knew better than to aim for the groin. His foot would have had to travel twice as far; give twice the time to dodge. And he doubted if such a kick would have been effective. The target was too small. The spot too vulnerable not to have been protected.

He felt something yield beneath the impact of his heavy boot. He let himself fall backwards, not fighting the natural movement, rolling as he hit the ground. He scrambled back on guard, ducked as a hand reached for his throat, winced as its companion slammed against his side. He backed quickly. Moidor followed him, stumbling as he rested his weight on his injured knee. Dumarest kicked again as the fighter gripped his shoulder. Moidor sucked in his breath.

'Quick,' he applauded. 'Vicious. You make a worthy opponent, my friend.' His hands clamped around Dumarest's throat. 'You have damaged my knee,' he purred. 'For that I shall not be kind. I will hurt you in return — badly. You will take a very long time to die.'

His hands began to close. Dumarest flung himself backwards, jerking up his knees and pressing them against the oiled barrel of the fighter's chest. He exerted the strength of his thighs, forcing himself backwards against the throttling hands. He was trying to utilize the whole power of his body against the strength of the fingers around his throat. Blood began to pound in his ears and his lungs to burn. Reaching up and back he found the little fingers. Taking one in each hand he pulled outwards, levering them from his throat.

Moidor opened his hands.

Impelled by the pressure of his thighs Dumarest fell backwards, landing heavily on his upper shoulders. He grunted as a naked foot, as hard as stone, kicked him in the side. He rolled as the same foot lashed at his kidneys. He staggered to his feet, the taste of blood in his mouth, sweat running into his eyes. He dashed it away, looking for the fighter. Moidor stood a few feet away, watching.

'A taste,' he said. 'Of what is to come.'

Dumarest gulped for breath. Red weals marked his throat and the shirt he had retained as protection against the fighter's nails hung in shreds. He dared not take the time to rip it off. Cautiously he backed, panting as he filled his lungs to oxygenate his blood. He circled so that his back was towards the sun.

Moidor lunged forward and stumbled.

'My knee!' His teeth shone in the cavern of his mouth. 'You will pay for that!'

He hopped forward and Dumarest moved barely in time. He stooped and snatched up a handful of dirt. He darted forward, hurling it into the snarling face, the gleaming eyes. He might as well have thrown a handful of mist.

He threw himself down and to one side as his rush carried him within reach of the fighter's grasp, his right hand hitting the dirt. He pivoted on his stiffened right arm, swinging his boot in a slashing arc towards the damaged knee. Bone yielded. Off-balance he tried to roll, to spin away from danger.

He was too slow. Moidor, balanced on one leg, caught him as he scrambled to his feet. Dumarest twisted as hands gripped his shoulders, slamming the edge of his palm across the fighter's nose. Blood spurted, mingling with the sweat and oil, staining the bared teeth vivid crimson.

'Now!' snarled Moidor. 'Now!'

His hands were steel traps as they closed on the biceps, the fingers digging in to rip the muscle from the bone. Dumarest groaned, tore himself free with the maniacal strength of desperation, flung himself behind the gleaming body. Savagely he kicked at the back of the uninjured knee.

Moidor fell.

Immediately Dumarest was on his back, one arm locked around his throat, knees grinding into his spine, his free hand clamped on his other wrist. He forced strength into his arms and shoulders and pulled upwards against the chin.

The watching crowd sucked in its breath.

He pulled harder. His ears began to sing and blackness edged his vision. From somewhere he could hear yells of encouragement but they sounded thin and distant. Beneath him Moidor stirred, hands groping at the dirt for leverage. A moment and he would be free. Dumarest lifted his eyes towards the sun. He heaved.

Bone snapped.

The sky turned the colour of blood.

6

The room was very quiet, very cool, the light soft and restful to the eyes. A faint scent of perfume hung in the air, gentling the more acrid odour of antiseptics, almost killing the elusive hint of spice. Something made tiny, metallic sounds to one side and he could hear the sound of breathing. Dumarest turned his head. A woman, no longer young, sat on a low stool before a squat machine. She was simply dressed in green, a caduceus emblazoned on her breast. She smiled as she saw the opened eyes.

'You are in the tents of the Matriarch of Kund,' she said. 'I am her personal physician. You are safe and have nothing to fear.'

She was efficient. She had answered his anticipated questions. Her voice was dry, a little precise but softer than he would have guessed. Dumarest looked past her at the soft hangings of the room, the thick carpet on the floor, the squat machine beside the couch. From it came the tiny, metallic clicking. The woman frowned. 'Did you understand what I said?'

'Yes.' Dumarest swallowed, surprised that he felt no pain. He touched his throat; it was unmarked, unswollen. He looked at his arm. It was covered by the sleeve of a shirt. The shirt was of a silken metallic fibre. He was fully dressed, even to his boots, but the clothes were not his own.

'You made no comment.'

'There was no need.' He sat upright and swung his legs over the side of the couch. 'I assume that I have been given some kind of medication.'

'You know?'

'I guessed.' He stretched, wondering a little at his feeling of well-being. He felt as he did after waking from a passage. He had been bathed, of course, and drugged and dressed in new clothes. He must also have been fed with intravenous injections of quickly-assimilated concentrates. He wondered why the old woman had treated him so well.

'The Matriarch is no lover of the

Prince of Emmened,' said the physician. She seemed able to read his mind or perhaps it was simply the extrapolation of the obvious. 'It pleased her to see his fighter die.'

'I killed him?'

'Yes.' She leaned forward a little, her eyes watchful. 'You remember?'

Dumarest nodded, wondering just what had happened after he'd made his final effort. Bone had snapped, that he could remember, and it must have been Moidor's neck. Then Megan had rushed forward his face distorted with excitement. But after?

'You were an automaton,' explained the woman. 'You stood and moved but without conscious awareness. The final exertion had thrown you into metabolic shock. You had overstrained your resources. Left alone you would have collapsed and, without proper treatment, could have died. The Matriarch recognized what had happened and took you under her protection.'

And, thought Dumarest grimly, had undoubtedly saved his life. The treatment he had needed was unavailable in camp and no one else would have risked the enmity of the prince by supplying it.

'How long have I been here?'

'I put you under slow-time. Subjectively you have been unconscious for a week. In actual time it has been a little under four hours.'

She turned to study the machine. Lights glowed from behind transparent windows, flickering to the rhythm of the metallic clicks, casting small splotches of colour over her face. Thoughtfully Dumarest massaged his throat. The equivalent of a week's skilled medication would more than account for his fitness. But slow-time was expensive. The old woman had been more than generous.

'I would like to see the Matriarch,' he told the physician. 'I want to give her my thanks for what she did.'

'That will not be necessary.'

'I think that it is.'

'What you think,' she said flatly, 'is of no real importance.' She did not turn from the machine. 'Later, if she should wish, you may have the opportunity of meeting her.'

Her meaning was crystal clear. He had been reminded that while the Matriarch ruled a complex of worlds he was nothing but a penniless traveller. Her generosity had been impersonal, the satisfying of a whim. She no more expected thanks from him than she would from a starving dog she had ordered to be fed.

The machine ceased its clicking. Stooping close the woman read the symbols in the transparent windows and frowned. Impatiently she pressed several buttons and slammed her hand on the release. The clicking began again, this time at a higher tempo.

'A diagnostic machine?' Dumarest had reason to be interested. She guessed his concern.

'Partially, yes. I have been giving you a routine check. You may be interested to learn that you have no contagious disease, virus infection, malignant growths or organic malfunction. Also that you have no trace of any foreign objects implanted in or on your body.' She hesitated. 'And I was totally unable to discover any sign of any post-hypnotic suggestion or mental conditioning impressed on your subconscious.'

He relaxed, smiling. 'Did that machine tell you all that?'

'That and more.' She glanced at the windows again as the machine fell silent. She frowned, then turned to face him. 'There are some questions I would like to ask. I have been studying your physique and encephalogram together with the constituents of your blood and your glandular secretions. I am somewhat puzzled. Where were you born?'

'Are you saying that I am not wholly human?'

Impatiently she brushed aside the suggestion. 'It isn't that. This machine contains the encoded data of all known physiology down to the molecular level. With the information I have introduced it should be able to tell me on which world you originated. It has failed to do so. Therefore the machine is either malfunctioning or you originated on a world of which it has no knowledge.' She paused. 'It is not malfunctioning.'

'Therefore, by your logic, I must

originate on a world of which it has no knowledge.' Dumarest smiled. 'Is that so incredible? There are countless inhabited worlds.'

'Not quite so many — and the machine embraces all that are known.'

Dumarest shrugged. 'Assuming that to be true — haven't you overlooked the possibility of mutation?'

'No. That is not the reason. What is the name of your native world?'

'Earth.'

She frowned, her lips thinning with anger. 'Please do not jest, I am serious. Many races so call the substance of their planet as they call it dirt or soil. What is the name of your primary?'

'Sol.'

'This is ridiculous!' She rose to her feet, insulted. 'I ask you the name of your sun and you reply with a word meaning exactly the same. Sun!' She almost spat the word. 'What sun?'

'The Sun.' He rose and smiled down at her, amused by her anger. 'I assure you that I am telling the truth.'

She snorted and left the room. After a

while he tried to follow and a guard blocked his passage. She was almost as tall as himself. Massive doses of testerone had accentuated her masculine characteristics. She faced him, one hand resting lightly on the butt of her holstered weapon.

'No.' Her voice was deep, as strong as her determination. 'You are to wait here.'

'Wait? For what?'

She didn't answer and Dumarest returned to the couch. He lay down, enjoying the softness of the bed, idly studying the motive on the ceiling. He had no objection to being detained in such luxurious surroundings.

* * *

The wine was a living emerald flecked with drifting motes of ruby. The goblet was blown from lustrous glass veined with gold. The sweat of condensation clung to the outside in minute droplets of moisture. The liquid was as frigid as polar ice.

'From Woten,' said the girl carelessly.

'You have been there?'

'No.' Dumarest sipped at the wine, feeling the chill of it bite his tongue, the potency of it sear his throat. Released by the warmth of his hand the bouquet rose to fill his nostrils with a cloying scent. 'It seems a rare vintage, my lady.'

'Many use it for perfume.' Seena Thoth was not interested in the wine. She left her own untouched as she sat facing her guest, her eyes roving over the hard planes of his face, the firm yet sensuous mouth. He seemed different from the ragged savage she had seen kill a man with his bare hands. 'You have travelled far?'

'Yes, my lady.' He wondered why he had been detained for her pleasure. To satisfy her curiosity, of course, but what else? 'I have been travelling most of my life. Ever since I left my home planet.'

'Earth?'

'Yes.' He caught her smile. 'I told the truth, my lady.'

'The physician does not think so.' She was not really interested in his planet of origin. 'You risked your life when you fought Emmened's creature,' she said

93

abruptly. 'What made you do it?'

'The prize, my lady.'

'A thing so small?' Her doubt was genuine. 'To risk your life?'

'Wealth is relative,' explained Dumarest patiently. It was obvious that she had never known the desperation of poverty. 'It is not a pleasant thing to be stranded on a world such as this.'

'But surely better to be stranded than to be dead? Moidor was a trained fighter of men. He killed the others as I would snap a twig.' Her eyes grew speculative. 'Are you also a trained fighter of men?'

'No, my lady.'

'Then you must have a secret skill. How else did you succeed when the others failed?'

'The others made a mistake.' Dumarest looked at her with critical eyes. She was as beautiful as the goblet, as exciting as the wine. The jewels she had braided in the ebon of her hair must have cost a hundred High passages. The ring on her finger the same. He grew thoughtful as he studied the ring. 'They thought it was a game and tried to win according to the rules. That was their mistake. It killed them. In combat there are no rules.'

'Is that why you kicked at his knee?' She smiled, remembering. 'I wondered why you had done that.'

'It is hard for a man, no matter how strong or well-trained, to stand on a broken leg. It gave me an advantage the others did not have.' Dumarest sipped more of his wine. He could have told her of his other great advantage over the men who had died. They had been conditioned under the benediction-light to respect the Supreme Ethic. They had entered the fight psychologically unable to kill. Instead he said; 'Have you ever killed, my lady?'

'No.'

'Or caused the death of others?'

'No.' She remembered a tortured face staring at an empty sky; blood on a cone of polished glass. 'No!'

He sensed her trouble and picked up her goblet of wine. 'You are not drinking, my lady.'

She waved aside the goblet. 'Tell me what it is to kill,' she demanded. 'Do dreams come to haunt your sleep? Do you regret having taken a life?'

He sipped wine, watching her over the rim of the goblet.

'Tell me,' she ordered. 'What is it like to hold a living creature in your hands and — '

'To kill it?' Dumarest turned and set down his glass. The base made a small sound as it hit the surface of the inlaid table. 'It is a matter of survival. You kill because you have no choice. Having no choice makes it unnecessary to regret the inevitable.'

He heard the sudden intake of breath and wondered if he had guessed wrongly. If she had wanted him to supply the vicarious thrill of blood and pain then he had failed. But she hadn't seemed like so many of her class, a depraved animal craving sexual stimulation — and liable to take an unpleasant revenge if she didn't get it. Then he saw her smile.

'You are right,' she said gratefully. 'The necessity of killing must be dictated by the needs of survival. I'm glad to hear you say it.'

He knew better than to ask or question what ghost he had lain to rest. She had wanted to meet a man who had risked his life for what she considered to be a trifle. She had expected nothing, an alleviation of boredom at the most, but Dumarest had surprised her with the impact of his personality. She found herself strangely reluctant to let him go.

He could have told her why. Despite her wealth and culture she had lived all her life in a narrow stratum of a single society. He had trod a hundred worlds, lived a varied life, seen a thousand things of interest. Seena was like the handler on his ship. Her walls were invisible but they existed just the same.

'You must have more wine,' she decided. 'Not that cold stuff from Woten but a warmer vintage from the slopes of Segalia on Kund.' She rose to fetch the flagon and fresh glasses. 'Have you ever been to Kund?'

'No, my lady.' He watched the grace of her movements across the floor, wondering why she hadn't called a servant to fetch the wine. As she poured he watched her hands.

'Here!' She handed him a glass with

her ringed hand. He took it, then looked sharply into her face. Her eyes were bright, her breathing rapid. 'We'll drink a toast,' she said. 'In celebration of your victory. To the dead — they won't bother us!'

Deliberately he set down the untouched wine.

'You don't like the toast?' She looked at the wine and then at his face. 'Is something wrong?'

'Your ring, my lady. It reminded me of something.'

'So?'

'You asked if I'd ever been to Kund,' he said evenly. 'I haven't, but I've been to Quail. They too have a matriarchy.'

She sat down, watching him.

'I had a very good friend on Quail. He attracted the attention of some rich and idle women. One of them wanted to have some fun and so she invited him to her house. She had her fun and then decided to have more. She accused him of rape.' He looked steadily into her eyes. 'Can you guess at the penalty for rape on a world like Quail?'

'Kund also protects its women.'

'Naturally. The man, of course, had no defence. The accusation was enough and they found what they regarded as conclusive evidence. So they removed his eyelids, his nose, lips, ears and tongue. They also made quite certain that he could never again be accused of the same crime. The woman attended the place of punishment.'

'As was her right as the victim.' Seena looked uncomfortable.

'I wonder.' Dumarest reached out and took her hand into his own. He touched the ring with the tip of one finger. 'She wore a ring exactly like this. I saw it at the trial. Later I learned that they are made by the artisans of the Kullambar sea. They are hollow and a slight pressure will release a little of their contents. Sometimes it is poison. The women of Quail get a great deal of sport from them. They fill them with a powerful aphrodisiac.'

He smiled and released her hand and, somehow, knocked over his wine.

In a room heavy with the scent of spice and rich with the brilliant tapestries spun by the spider-folk of a distant star an old woman spoke softly to her mirror.

'Mirror, mirror, on the wall — who is the fairest of us all?'

Once it had been Gloria's pleasure to have the mechanism respond in terms of the purest flattery to the fragment of verse half-learned as a child. Now the sonic lock no longer pandered to her conceit. The surface clouded as the scanners sought their target. It cleared to show the diminished figures of Dumarest and her ward. He was telling her the story of his friend.

Gloria thinned her lips as she heard it, wondering if Seena recognized the implied insult. Probably not. The girl needed the help of no drugs to find herself a lover but she couldn't blame the man for his caution. She knew of the harridans of Quail and their spiteful ways. It was natural for him to be suspicious. She nodded as he spilled the wine.

'A clever man, my lady.'

Dyne stood behind her, the scarlet of his robe subdued against the vivid tapestries. He had thrown back his cowl and his shaven head glowed in the soft lighting. Gloria shrugged.

'Clever, but safe.'

'Are you certain as to that, my lady?'

'He's clean inside and out. Melga made sure of that before I allowed Seena to venture into his reach. She is bored and needs someone to amuse her. Dumarest is more capable than most and safer than any.' She looked at the screen. They sat close as he told her a story of his travelling. Now, she noticed, he did not hesitate to drink the wine. But then she thought cynically, he had poured it himself.

For a moment she wished that she were young again so that she could teach him how hard it was for any man to resist a determined woman.

'I am not sure that I trust him, my lady.' Dyne looked thoughtfully at the screen. 'It could have been arranged for him to be here at this time.'

'How?' She was impatient with his excessive caution. 'He rode with us by accident — I have checked with the handler of our ship. And his fight with

Moidor, that was real enough. He would have died had I not taken him under my protection. Could he or anyone have anticipated that?'

'Perhaps not,' admitted the cyber. 'But there is something mysterious about him.'

'His planet of origin?' She looked sidewise and up at the tall figure. 'Didn't Melga tell you? He claimed to have originated on Earth.'

'Earth?'

'Yes. Melga thought he was having a joke at her expense and he probably was. She was not amused, but then she lacks humour. If he wants to keep the planet of his origin a secret why not allow him his mystery?' She smiled at the figures on the screen. 'A strange person,' she murmured. 'And no fool.' She snapped her fingers and the scene dissolved, the mirror returning to a plain, reflecting surface. 'Is everything progressing as planned?'

'Yes, my lady. I have arranged to hire bearers from the camp. The factor tells me that such work is their only means of employment. The dispersal of the guards is as agreed.'

'And the ship?'

'The captain has his orders. He will not fail.'

'If he does he will pay for it if I have to offer a principality for his head!' For a moment naked cruelty showed from beneath the cultured facade. It vanished as the Matriarch turned to other matters. 'You think, then, that we are safe?'

'I cannot be sure, my lady.' He met the sudden anger of her eyes. 'I am not infallible. When the subject was mentioned I gave certain advice. It was the best means possible to achieve the desired end. But I cannot be certain beyond all question of doubt. There is always the unknown factor.'

'An excuse?'

'An explanation, my lady.' Her anger left him unmoved. 'Would you have me lie? If so, then I am not needed here. Any courtier could do as much.'

She looked away, conscious of her helplessness as far as he was concerned. Anger, promises, threats, all were useless against a machine. She could dismiss him and that was the full extent of her power.

If she did more the Cyclan would take their revenge.

But always remained the tiny seed of suspicion. The shadow of doubt. Advice, like luck, could be of two kinds.

'Is there anything more, my lady?' Dyne was anxious to be gone. Cynically she wondered why.

'No.' She dismissed him with a gesture, waiting until he had left the room before daring to relax. Then she sighed, her shoulders rounding with fatigue. At times like this she felt her age. Felt too the waves of savage ambition threatening the things she loved. They were few enough.

Her palace on Kund. A small garden, some jewels, a lock of once-bright hair. The Lady Seena.

A small showing for a lifetime of rule.

She whispered at the mirror and again it showed Dumarest and her ward. They had not moved from the room. Their movements had been in space and time. The girl was a little flushed and seemed to have grown even more feminine as she sat close to the traveller. So close that he could not help but breathe the scent of

104

her perfume. The Matriarch nodded her approval.

Dyne had his cold predictions based on known data and logical extrapolation, but she had better than that. She had the age-old intuition of her sex which could confound all logic. She had relied on it to carry her along a bloodstained path to the throne. She relied on it to safeguard her ward.

Her face softened as she looked at the girl, feeling the bittersweet tug of memory, the determination to protect her at any cost. The man could be of use in that despite the cyber's doubts. What did he know of the magical power of emotion?

The old woman smiled as she looked at the couple then the smile froze on her face. She felt a sudden pounding of her heart, the terrible paralysis induced by overwhelming fear. The couple were no longer alone.

Death had joined the party.

7

It came on a blur of shimmering wings, a thin, finger-long body tipped with triangular jaws strong enough to shear through metal, to penetrate the toughest hide. It ripped through the plastic of the room, poised for a moment in the corner, then swept towards where the couple sat.

Dumarest saw it barely in time. The Lady Seena was very close, her perfume an enticing scent in his nostrils, the warm, white velvet of her flesh radiating its feminine heat. She was attentive and had a trick of staring into his face as if seeing there something special to herself. Cynicism kept him detached. Such a woman would be sated with empty flattery and the easy conquest of desirous males. She was only amusing herself, unable to resist the challenge of his maleness, playing an age-old game with tired indifference.

So he told himself, and managed to negate her charm.

'In your travels,' she said softly, 'you must have met many women. Tell me of them.'

'Is that an order, my lady?'

'No. You will tell?'

'No. I — ' He sensed rather than saw the darting shape and reacted by pure instinct. 'Down!'

She screamed as he threw himself against her, knocking her from her chair, sending them both to the carpet. There was a thin whine, a faint *plop* as the thing hit the wall behind them, merging instantly into the background with a chameleon-like change of protective body-tint.

'Guards!' She thought that he had attacked her, that he was intent on rape. He rapped a command.

'Shut up! Listen!'

He rose, crouching, eyes scanning the wall. A patch of colour flickered and he flung himself down, throwing his weight hard against the woman, rolling her over the carpet. Again came the thin, spiteful hum, the soft *plop* of landing. His ears caught the sound and directed his eyes. He reached behind him and groped for a chair. He found one and clamped his fingers around the backrest.

Something flickered on the wall.

He swept up the chair, holding it as a shield as he lunged towards the woman. Something tugged at his hair. He spun, feeling sweat bead his face, eyes searching the wall. He caught a glimpse of a jewelled eye before it vanished into the background. He watched the spot. The thing was fast; too fast for the eye to follow once it was in flight. The only chance was to intercept it before it struck.

'What is it?' Seena half-rose from her knees, her initial fear forgotten. 'I can't see — '

'Shut up!'

He caught the shift of colour and jerked up the chair just in time. The thing hit the seat, drilled through, scored a deep groove across the backrest and caromed off the metal-fabric of his shirt. Its wings a tattered ruin, it threshed on the carpet, then scuttled forward on multiple legs.

Dumarest crushed it beneath the heel of his boot.

'A phygria,' said Melga. The physician was very pale. She had come running at the heels of the guards. 'You recognized it?'

'No.' Dumarest looked at the chair still in his hand. The scar on the backrest almost touched the skin. He set down the chair and looked at the corner of the room. A hole gaped in the plastic. 'I saw something move,' he explained. 'The rest was instinct.'

'You must have very unusual reflexes,' said the physician thoughtfully. 'The attack speed of a phygria is over fifty miles an hour. That would give you — ' she paused, measuring the room with calculating eyes, 'about a third of a second to see it, recognize its danger and to have taken the necessary action based on that recognition. You know of them?'

'Yes.'

'That would account for your subconscious recognition. You simply didn't have the time for conscious thought.' She stooped, picked up the crushed body in a pair of forceps, examined it through a glass. 'A female, gravid, searching for a host.' Her lips tightened. 'A human is not its natural host. That means — '

'It was primed,' said Dumarest harshly. He looked down at his hands, they were trembling a little from reaction. He remembered the tug at his hair, the scar close to his hand. Death had twice come very close. 'It was primed,' he repeated. 'We all know what that means.'

He looked at the beauty of the girl and wondered who wanted her dead.

★ ★ ★

Gloria was tormented by the same thought. A phygria was an assassin's weapon. Primed with the scent of the victim it would unerringly seek out the target to use as its host. Like a bullet it would smash through the skin into the flesh beneath there to vomit forth a gush of tiny eggs. Swept by the bloodstream they would scatter throughout the body there to hatch and grow. Too numerous for surgical removal, too tough for chemical destruction, they would bring an inevitable and horrifying end.

The thought of Seena dying, the unwilling host to a thousand hungry larvae, made her want to retch.

'Who?' she snarled at the cyber standing at her side. 'Who would want to kill her on this god-forsaken planet?'

It was a stupid question but she was too distraught to realize it. An assassin needed no reason other than his pay but Dyne didn't remind her of that. Instead he countered her question with another.

'Not who, my lady, but how? The phygria was primed — how did the assassin obtain her scent?'

The old woman snorted her impatience. It was simple enough, a clipping from a nail, a strand of hair, some perspiration, a trace of blood — there were a dozen ways in which a host could be identified. Then she grew thoughtful as his meaning penetrated her anger and fear. Seena was guarded, isolated from common contact. To be effective a scent had to be reasonably fresh. She felt the sudden chill of her blood, the overwhelming weight of despair but the possibility had to be faced.

'Treason?'

'It is a possibility,' he admitted, 'but of a very low order of probability. It seems impossible that there could be a traitor in your retinue.'

'Seems?'

'No human action can be predicted to one hundred per cent certainty, my lady. But there is an alternative explanation. The target need not have been the Lady Seena.'

'Dumarest?'

'Yes, my lady. From the evidence it seems that the phygria attacked him, not the Lady Seena. He naturally assumed that she was the target but he could have been wrong. The probability is high that he was. His scent would not have been difficult to obtain.'

'From Moidor?'

'Yes, my lady, or from his discarded clothing.' Dyne paused. 'We can even guess the motive.'

She nodded. It made sense and the Prince of Emmened was known to be a vengeful man. It would be like him to avenge the death of his favourite and simple if he had the means at hand. And yet it all seemed to fit too neatly. She had long since learned to distrust neat solutions to important problems.

'In my view,' said Dyne, 'it would be wise to ensure that he never again comes into close contact with the Lady Seena. The risk, if he is the target of an assassin, would be too great.'

He echoed her thoughts but, by echoing them, stiffened her earlier resolution. Dumarest had proved his worth and Seena could do with the protection of such a man. And, despite the cyber's logical explanation, she still had doubts. The possibility of treachery could not be overlooked.

A communicator chimed, a fairy-bell in the spice-scented chamber. She threw the switch. Melga stared at her from the screen.

'My lady,' she said, and paused waiting for the Matriarch to speak.

'Well?' The old woman had little use for protocol in times of emergency. 'Did you isolate the scent?'

'No, my lady. It was impossible to

distinguish who was the actual target.'

It was a disappointment; she had hoped the physician could have settled the matter and guided her into appropriate action. Now there was only one thing to be done.

'Nullify them both.' She broke the connection and sat brooding over the set. She reached for a button then hesitated. It wouldn't take long for the physician to inject both Dumarest and her ward with scent-masking chemicals but they would have to be guarded until all danger from further attacks was past. Deciding, she pressed the button.

'My lady?' Elspeth, the captain of her guard, looked from the screen.

'Prepare for departure. We leave in two hours.'

'For the north, my lady?'

'For the north.'

* * *

The tourist was in a flaming temper. He slammed his hand on the counter hard enough to bruise the flesh. If there was

114

pain he ignored it.

'Listen,' he snapped. 'I was given to understand that you would look after me. I haven't come all this way to be given the brush-off. If you can't do your job here then your main office ought to know about it and I'm the man to tell them. Now tell me just why I can't hire a plane.'

'Because there isn't one on the planet.' Piers Quentin fought the jumping of his nerves. For the past two hours, ever since the Matriarch of Kund had left Hightown, his office had resembled a madhouse. 'There's no need for them,' he explained. 'The only place anyone wants to see is the mountains and they aren't far. You could walk it comfortably in a couple of days.'

'Walk?' The man purpled. 'Walk!'

'Or you could hire a nulgrav raft,' said the factor quickly. 'I think that there is one left.' There wasn't, but someone would have to double-up. 'An appreciation of the scenery is an integral part of the attraction,' he continued. 'Mechanical noise would disrupt the harmony and ruin what you have come so far to experience. You can hire bearers to carry supplies and to provide motive power, of course. I assure you, sir, it is the normal custom for people like yourself.'

The man grumbled but allowed himself to be convinced. He grumbled even louder at the hiring costs. Piers spread his hands at the objections.

'I can't help it, sir. The bearers are free agents who will not work for less. The supplies are on sale or return and there is a deposit on the raft. If you will sign here, sir, and here. Thank you. If you take this slip to the warehouse the quartermaster will attend to your needs.'

He relaxed as the man left the office, relaxing still more as he realized that the man was the last. Outside would still be chaos but his staff could handle that. Now he was going to shut the door and take a long, cold drink. Brother Ely smiled at him as he was about to close the panel.

'Alone, brother?'

'I was,' said Piers shortly, then relented. 'Come in and keep me company. I've had a hell of a time this past few hours.' He closed the door after the monk and crossed to the dispenser. 'Something to drink? No. Well, you won't mind if I do.' He helped himself regardless and downed the drink in two long swallows. 'The old woman started it,' he said waiting for a refill. 'I told them all that she was far too early but they wouldn't listen. Not that it matters, at least they're out of my hair now.'

'And, of course,' said the monk quietly, 'they will use more than normal supplies in order to maintain their bearers and themselves. There is no water by the mountains?'

'No.'

'Nor food?'

'No — everything has to be carried.' The factor tasted his second drink. 'Food, water, tents — everything. The Hightowners ride on rafts which the bearers pull along. It works pretty well.'

For himself, naturally, but it went deeper than that. There was a perversity in human nature which gloried at the bestialisation of its own kind. There was a romance clinging to the concept of slavery which appealed to the rich. They would like to ride high and move by the muscle-power of desperate men. As the factor well knew, those who had started by demanding planes would end by regretting the loss of slaves. Their use gave a sense of personal power lacking in the employment of machines.

Brother Ely knew that only too well. He said one word loaded with contempt. 'Pander!'

'What!' The factor jerked so that some of the drink spilled from his glass. 'What did you call me?'

The monk repeated it. Quentin set down his glass. He crossed to the door, opened it, pointed outside. His face was white with rage beneath the dark pattern of his beard. 'Get out!'

Deliberately the monk looked for a chair, found one, sat down. 'Spare me your outraged pride, brother. We both know exactly what I mean by the word. Why did you remove the engines from the rafts? Such craft normally contain their own motive power. Are you trying to add to the attractions of Gath?'

Irritably Quentin slammed the door

and returned to his drink. The old monk was shrewd but much good would it do him.

'What would you have me do?' Quentin swallowed the rest of his drink. 'The tourists are rich and to travel so is a novelty they appreciate. And it gives work to the travellers. Without it they would starve.'

'Do they have to lower themselves to the level of beasts of burden in order to live?'

'That is your judgement,' snapped Quentin irritably. 'Perhaps they do not think the same. A starving man cannot afford the niceties of your ethics. At least,' he added spitefully, 'they do not beg.'

'And we of the Universal Brotherhood do,' said the monk gently. He smiled. 'I take your point, brother.'

Piers was not amused. He had done nothing beyond the scope of his duties and had to answer to no one but his superiors. But the Brotherhood had friends in peculiar places. He stood to lose nothing by caution.

'What's on your mind?' The factor

helped himself to another drink. He felt a little sorry for himself. No sooner had he rid himself of the incubus of the storm than this had to happen. 'What did you want to talk about?'

'Shall we begin with Dumarest?'

'The man who killed the Prince of Emmened's fighter? What of him?'

'Has the wager been paid?'

'The price of a High passage is in my keeping.'

'And if Dumarest should die?' The monk didn't wait for an answer. 'He has no one to call you to account. You would keep the money.'

Piers didn't answer.

'A quick way to make a tidy sum,' mused the old man. 'More. If Dumarest should die you would be free of a man you may have reason to fear.'

Piers laughed in the monk's face. 'Brother, you're crazy! I have no need to kill Dumarest for the reason you mention. He will leave on the first ship. His passage is assured. Why should I want him dead?'

'Greed.' Ely was bland as he looked at the factor. 'You are a greedy man, brother. It is a carnal sin and could prove fatal.' His lifted hand stilled the other's protest. 'I do not threaten but simply point out the obvious. You cannot be certain that Dumarest will leave Gath on a High passage. He is strong and accustomed to travelling Low. He might choose to take others with him. The strongest, naturally, only they could survive. Could you spare so many willing bearers, brother?'

'I'll be glad to see them go. All of them.' Piers gulped at his drink. 'The penniless scum! The sooner they go the better!'

'So you keep saying — I don't believe you.' The monk grew stern. 'Let us not fence with words, brother. You set the fee for their hiring. You put the price on their food. You know that every penny they earn will find its way into your pocket. You may not have initiated the system but you are taking full advantage of it. Brother, I would not have your conscience for the wealth of a world.'

'There is an old saying,' said Piers quietly. 'The man who rides a tiger finds

121

it difficult to dismount.'

'He could have help, brother.'

'At a price?'

'There is always a price,' admitted the old monk. 'Sometimes it is more than a man is willing to pay. Pride is a great sin, brother. Do not let it blind you.'

Piers finished his drink and slowly mixed himself another, taking time over the adjustment of alcohol, flavouring and ice. He stood, looking through the window at the scene beyond. It depressed him even more.

'They arrive with every ship,' he said flatly. 'One, two, sometimes as many as six or seven at a time. They have next to nothing when they land. There is nothing here they can gain. Some die but always there are others to take their place.'

'And you are alone with but a handful of guards,' said the monk.

'Yes,' admitted the factor. He turned and looked at Ely. 'What do you want? Facilities for a church in Hightown? You can have them, but what good it will do I don't know. It is hard to preach ethics to those who value nothing but money. A church in Lowtown? You can have that too and I'll put you and your monks on the roster for regular food. You may break your hearts but you won't starve.' Piers swallowed the last of his drink. 'Who knows? You may even be able to persuade them to be content with their lot. What else you can do I can't imagine.'

'Perhaps you underestimate the power of the Brotherhood,' said the monk evenly. 'It is not beyond speculation that the travellers might take a hand in their own destiny. Who then would tend the field, clear the path, act as bearers for the tourists who come to Gath?'

'A union?' The factor made no secret of his disgust. 'Are you threatening me with that? A man of your calling to deal in a thing so vile!'

'By the pattern on your face I see that you belong to a guild,' said the monk sharply. 'What else is that but a union of people engaged in serving their common end?'

Quentin shrugged. He could see no relationship between the professional guild of which he was a member and a union of unspecialized types, the thought of which aroused only disgust. Professional men had ethics; the others did not.

'I do not seek to threaten you,' said Ely quietly. 'The Brotherhood does not threaten, but this I must know. Are you against us?'

'Certainly not.'

'You will permit us then to help the unfortunate?'

'Of course.' Piers had nothing to lose and much to gain. The enmity of the Brotherhood was to be avoided and, if trouble should arise, he would have someone to blame.

'I am glad to hear you say it.' The old monk's face expressed his joy. 'The Brotherhood has always striven for the greatest good for the greatest number while maintaining established rule. Here it would take so little. A simple adjustment of the fees charged the tourists. A system to provide and distribute natural food. Some medical care — we are good at such things. We shall rid you of your tiger, brother. Never fear.'

8

They camped half-way to the mountains, an irregular sprawl of rafts and tents and weary travellers. The rafts had no weight, their nulgrav plates kept them on a level three feet above the ground, but they had mass and had to be towed every inch of the way.

It was growing darker, the air dim and filled with shadows as the path swept towards the eternal night of the east. The sun had almost vanished beneath the horizon, only the upper rim remaining visible, painting the west with the colour of blood. The air was heavy, brooding, filled with invisible forces. Above, the pale light of stars shone in a purple sky.

Megan groaned with the pain of his shoulders. He eased the clothing from his back and cursed in a low monotone. He looked up as a tall figure occluded the sky and spoke his name.

'Megan?'

'Is that you, Dumarest?' Megan tried to stand, groaned, made a second attempt. He relaxed as the tall man knelt beside him.

'What's the matter with you? Are you hurt?'

'My back.' Megan winced. 'Could you get me some salve or something? That Emmened!'

'I heard.' Dumarest's hands were gentle as they bared the thin shoulders. He stared grimly at the welts criss-crossing the pallid flesh. 'You fool, Megan! Why did you take service with him? You had enough money to take this trip easy.'

'It isn't my money.'

'So what? There's more than I need. You didn't have to get yourself half-killed for the sake of a few units.'

'I need the money.' Megan was stubborn and Dumarest could appreciate his pride. 'How was I to know the devil would use the whip?'

It had been a hell of a trip. The Prince of Emmened, savage at having been left behind in the rush to follow the Matriarch, had tried to make up time and forge to the lead. His method had been simple. Order the towing travellers to run and whip them until they obeyed.

And continue whipping them all the way to the present camp.

His guards had helped but the fear of being left behind without employment had helped even more. Starvation, as the factor had cynically pointed out, made ethics and pride of minor consideration to food. Even so two had died and five had been left on the journey.

'You've finished working for him.' Dumarest had salve, he applied it with a gentle hand. 'Don't worry about losing your money. You don't need it. None of you need it. I've enough to buy off all his bearers. He can use his guards and courtiers to pull instead.'

'That's stupid.' Megan relaxed as the pain in his shoulders yielded to the soothing action of the salve. 'Do that and you'll get yourself killed. You can't treat a man like the prince that way and you know it.'

It was the truth but none the more palatable because of that. Dumarest had the money but it wasn't enough. He needed more than money. He needed the power and protection he didn't have.

'All right,' he admitted. 'So we forget the others. But don't let me see you working for Emmened again.'

He rose and left the other man, wandering over the camp, feeling restless with unvented anger. A group of travellers sat around a blanket rolling dice for their day's pay. The cubes clicked and bounced and called forth groans and cheers as they came to rest. Someone would be the winner but, in the end, there could only be one man who collected the money. Quentin would take it all.

His irritation grew. Striking out he left the camp, walking towards the night side, his feet noiseless in the grass. He walked for almost a mile and then dropped as he saw dim figures in the gloom. Hugging the grass he watched them pass. Four of them, tall, broad, masculine even in the way in which they walked. He wondered why the guards of the Matriarch should be so far from camp. A routine patrol, perhaps, but what danger to their ruler could be on Gath?

He was thoughtful on his return to camp.

The place had a festive air. Small fires glowed in the ruby dusk and the scent of cooking food reached his nostrils. The scent stimulated his appetite. Megan would have food or he could get some from the kitchens of the Matriarch. He could even buy food which had been stolen from the tourists — for this brief time they were fair game. He lengthened his stride.

And almost died beneath the blaze of a laser.

★   ★   ★

Luck saved him. A tufted root twisted beneath his foot and threw him to one side, away from the blast of energy which came from behind. Common sense kept him alive. He continued to fall, letting his body grow limp, hitting the ground face down, pressing the left side of his head against the grass so that its supposed injury was hidden, masking the right side with an upflung arm. He remained motionless, not moving even when the whisper of footsteps came very close. They halted, too far away for him to reach, and he held his breath.

The footsteps moved a little closer.

The scent of the grass was in his nostrils, the damp odour of the ground. A stone dug cruelly into his side and the tingling between his shoulders grew almost unbearable but he knew that to move was to die. The assailant was watching, reluctant, perhaps, to attract attention with a second shot, but certain to fire again in case of need. Then, after an eternity, the footsteps rustled away.

Dumarest waited a long time before he rolled and sat upright.

He was alone. No silhouette blocked the sky, no shape stood in near-invisibility against the purple of the east. He could see nothing but the loom of tents and the tiny glow of fires bright against the red-stained sky of the west. Whoever had fired had vanished as quietly as he had come. Or as she had come. There was no way to tell.

Dumarest wondered who had wanted him dead.

The guards, perhaps? One could have spotted him and have circled to cut him down and shut his mouth. A creature of the Prince of Emmened seeking revenge for the death of his favourite? A traveller bribed by the factor to burn him down so that he could keep his passage money? There was no way of telling.

The camp had settled down by the time he returned. Weary figures hugged the ground, watchful figures guarded the tents, the tourists had gathered in little clumps for company and mutual protection. One of them waved to Dumarest as he passed. He was a smooth, rosily fat man wearing bright clothes and with a peculiarly marked ring on his finger.

'Hey, friend, care for a game?'

'Of what?' Dumarest halted, wondering if they knew who he was. His dress was not that of the other travellers.

'You name it, we'll play it.' The man riffled a deck of cards. 'Highest, lowest, man-in-between. Best guess — straight or two out of three. Starmash, olkay, nine-card nap. Your choice, friend.' The cards made a dry rattling as he passed them from one hand to the other. 'Come close and have a drink.'

'I'll take the drink.' After his narrow escape Dumarest felt that he could do with it. The gambler handed him a bottle and he lifted it to his lips. He swallowed a gulp of a full three ounces. It was good liquor. 'Thanks.' He handed back the bottle. The man's eyes widened as he took it.

'Say, I know you! You're the one who beat the prince's fighter. Man, that was a real treat. Something I wouldn't have wanted to miss.' He became confidential. 'Listen, if you want to turn professional I could fix you up all the way.'

'No.'

'Maybe you're right.' The gambler wasn't annoyed at the abrupt refusal. 'A pro gets known too fast. Tell you what. Let me handle things. I know quite a few places that have a liking for blood. We can kid them to back their local and then you step in. Get it? Just like you did with Moidor but this time you'd get plenty of gravy.' He chuckled. 'I forgot. You didn't do so bad; a High passage is plenty of loot for a — ' He broke off. Dumarest finished the sentence.

'For a stranded bum of a penniless traveller?' His voice was very gentle. 'Is that what you were going to say?'

'No!' The man was sweating. 'Look, no offence. Have another drink.'

'I'll cut you for a double handful of units,' said Dumarest. He leaned close so that the man could see his eyes. 'High man wins.' He watched the deft way in which the gambler shuffled the cards. 'I've got the feeling that I'm going to win,' he said evenly. 'It's a pretty strong feeling. I'll be very annoyed if it's wrong.'

He won. He wasn't surprised. He wasn't ashamed either of the way he had forced the result. A man had to pay for having a loose mouth. The gambler had got off cheap.

He left the tourists and headed across the camp, carefully stepping over slumbering figures huddled around the fires. A small line had formed where the Brothers Angelo and Benedict had set up their portable church and he wondered at the energy of the monks. His eyes narrowed as he found what he was looking for. Sime, apparently fast asleep, rested beside his coffin.

Dumarest looked around. It was still too bright for him to be totally unobserved if anyone were watching but details would be blurred by the dim light. He dropped to one knee very close to the sleeping man. His hand touched the coffin and he leaned forward — and saw the gleam of watchful eyes.

'Sime?'

'What is it?' The man lifted himself on one elbow. His gaunt chest was bare beneath the ragged tatters of his shirt, his face skeletal in the ruby glow. 'What do you want?'

'I've got a proposition.' Dumarest leaned close so that the man could smell the liquor on his breath. 'Remember me? I helped you carry this thing from the field.' His hand rapped the coffin.

'I remember.'

'Well, I can get you a lift with it. A couple of units will do it.'

'No.'

'Are you stupid? We've got as far again to go. You want to pass out before we reach the mountains?'

'No, of course not.'

'Then how about it?' Dumarest sounded impatient. 'A couple of units to one of the guards and he'll load it on a raft. It's worth it.'

'Thank you, but no.'

'What's the matter? Short of cash?' Dumarest reached towards his pocket. 'I can lend it to you if you like.'

'It isn't that.' Sime reared upright and rested one arm on the lid of the box. 'I know you mean well but it's a personal matter. Please try to understand.'

Dumarest shrugged. 'Suit yourself — it's your funeral.'

He rose to his feet, half-turned and caught a glimpse of movement. He lurched towards it and almost trod on the recumbent body of the old crone who had travelled with Sime. She appeared to be fast asleep.

★ ★ ★

Melga adjusted the hypogun and held the nozzle close to the furry hide of a small animal which Dyne held securely in his hands. It was one of a dozen she had brought with her from Kund. She watched it for a moment then pressed the trigger. Air blasted a charge of anaesthetic through the hide and into the blood-stream. Immediately the animal went limp.

'A routine experiment?' asked the cyber, 'or are you merely killing time?'

'A little of both,' she said shortly. Taking the animal from his hands she fastened it to the surface of the dissecting table. 'This is a routine precautionary measure,' she explained. 'The animal has been sensitized to be extremely vulnerable to any and all forms of disease which could possibly threaten a human.' She sat down, picked up a heavy scalpel and bared the skull with a few, deft strokes. 'Soon we shall be within sight of the mountains,' she continued. 'The winds will be from the east. It is barely possible that they could carry harmful substances. If so some residue could remain in this

136

area. I dare take no chances if I am to protect the Matriarch and her ward.'

The cyber nodded. 'And others?'

'Those too.' She cut and snipped and discarded. A saw whined briefly as it sliced through bone. A suction device removed the top of the skull. Expertly she probed the mass of tissue, baring the innermost recesses of the creature's brain. He caught the sound of her indrawn breath.

'Something?'

'No.'

She put down the probe and picked up a scalpel. Quickly she stripped the rest of the hide from the now-dead creature. Again she cut and delved, this time with more speed but no less skill. Finally she put aside her instruments and leaned back in her chair.

'Well?' The cyber was curious.

'Nothing,' she said flatly. Her voice was heavy with fatigue.

'The area is amazingly sterile.'

Reaching forward she pressed the release. The disposable top-sheet of the dissecting table sprang from the edges into a cup cradling the unwanted remains. She threw it into a disposal unit. A gush of blue flame converted it to ash.

Dyne narrowed his eyes against the brief glare. 'The storms could be responsible,' he suggested. 'There must be great releases of energy coupled with high-frequency sound. The vegetation could adapt but animal life is more delicate.'

'That could be the reason,' she admitted. She was acutely conscious of the confines of the tent, the clutter of her equipment. She was a tidy woman and such confusion caused her mental irritation. Dyne didn't help. He stood, a watchful figure, to one side of the table, the dissecting light casting hollows beneath his eyes. She wished that he would go away. She always worked better alone.

She closed her eyes, feeling waves of fatigue rolling over her like the waves of a sea, remotely conscious of the dull ache in her hands and wrists. Once it would not have been like this. Once she had been able to sit at her table and work and work and work . . . She caught herself on the edge of sleep and opened her eyes to the glare. Age, she thought wryly. It comes to us all.

She looked up and met the eyes of the cyber.

'You are tired,' he said. 'I had better go.'

'Yes,' she admitted. 'I am tired.' For a moment she envied him his apparent ability to do without sleep. She herself had hardly slept at all since they had arrived on Gath and now even drugs were losing their power to keep her awake. And a tired brain, as she knew, was no defence for the Matriarch.

9

The path veered more to the east so that the upper rim of the sun fell below the horizon and only a dull, red glow shone from beneath the sea. The stars were brighter now, limning the bulk of the mountains which waited ahead, casting a thin ghost-light on the grass and boulders to either side. Far below, from the base of the cliffs, the muted roar of the waves sounded like the pounding of a monstrous heart.

Gloria hated the sound. She sat beneath the canopy of her raft and felt her own heart pick up the rhythm and adjust to its tempo. It was too slow. It was like one of the punishments of old Kund in which the slowing beat of a mechanical drum had thrown its victims into catatonia. She felt her blood grow turgid, her thoughts dull. Irritably she sniffed at her pomander and concentrated on other things. On the line of the column stretching behind; the shorter line reaching ahead. The Prince of Emmened was in the van, no longer whipping his bearers now that he was in the lead. The lights on his rafts shone like miniature stars.

Abruptly she felt the need of company, of a voice to break the closing circle of her introspection. Imperiously she called to a guard.

'My Lady?' The guard was immediately attentive.

'A moment.' Gloria brooded, wondering whom to summon. Melga would have been her first choice but the physician was asleep, lying in one of the tented rafts, saline and glucose dripping into her veins, the magic of slow-time adding to her therapy. The fool of a woman had been almost dead from want of rest. Seena? Her ward had left the column, too bored to ride longer on the raft. Who else then? Gloria sighed, not for the first time feeling the loneliness of command. 'Dyne,' she decided. 'Call the cyber to attend me.'

He came within minutes, his face shielded by his cowl, the scarlet of his robe the colour of congealed blood in the dim light. He stood at her side and a little to the rear. His voice was as emotionless as ever.

'You sent for me, my lady?'

'Sit down,' she snapped. 'Keep me company. Talk.'

'Yes, my lady.' He had been resting but his voice did not betray the fact. He looked at the cavalcade, the combination of pomp and pride and poverty unique to Gath. 'An unusual sight, my lady.'

The Matriarch was unimpressed. 'There are better,' she said. 'The installation of a matriarch of Kund is a sight I have yet to see equalled.'

'Naturally, my lady.'

'You doubt?'

'No, my lady. But this spectacle is of nature rather than man.'

He lifted his face to the heavy air. The tension had increased so that it lay like a hot, crackling blanket over the area. Wisps of electrical energy glowed at the tips of metallic protuberances. The air wavered a little so that objects seen in the distance became distorted as if seen through inferior glass. It was as if they were all moving steadily towards new and unfamiliar dimensions.

The Matriarch shifted uneasily in her chair. The air, the pounding of the waves, the weird lighting, rested gratingly on her nerves. 'Talk,' she commanded. 'Talk.'

*   *   *

On a knoll towards the east of the curving path the Lady Seena stood and watched the slow progress of the column. She had become bored with riding and had chosen to walk. Chosen, too, Dumarest to walk with her but they were not alone. The Matriarch had seen to that. Beyond earshot but very much alert, a circle of guards accompanied the couple.

'It looks like a snake,' said the girl. She looked at the light-studded column etched against the dull red glow of the western sky. 'Or a centipede. Or an eltross from Vootan. They are composed of seven distinct types of creature united in a common symbiosis.'

Dumarest made no comment. His eyes were searching the column. He could see

143

the Brothers Angelo and Benedict, the structure of their portable church twin mounds on their shoulders. The laden figure of Sime, his burden grotesque in the midst of the carnival-like throng, crept steadily along to one side. He could not see the old crone.

'That man!' Seena pointed to Sime. 'What does he carry?' Dumarest told her. She stared her amazement. 'A coffin containing the dead body of his wife? You must be joking.'

'No, my lady.'

'But why?'

'He is probably very attached to her,' he said dryly. 'I understand that some men do feel that way about their wives.'

'Now I know that you are joking.' Seena was impatient. 'It is hardly a subject for jest.'

'I am not joking, my lady. It is common knowledge among the travellers.' He looked thoughtfully at the laden figure. 'I will admit that it is unusual to find a man so attached to a woman as is Sime.'

'But why?' The question bothered her. 'Why did he bring her to Gath?'

'That is the question, my lady.' Dumarest looked at the woman at his side. 'I am not sure as to his reason but there is a legend on Earth that, at the very last day, a trumpet will sound and all the dead shall rise to live again. Perhaps he hopes to hear the sound of that trumpet — or that his wife shall hear it.'

'But she is dead.'

'Yes, my lady.'

'But — ' She frowned her irritation. 'You fail to make sense,' she complained. 'I have heard of no such legend.'

'The Brothers would enlighten you, my lady.'

'Have they also been to Earth?' She laughed at his expression. 'No, how could they? Do you really expect me to believe there is such a place?'

'You should — it is very real.' He began walking so as to keep abreast of the Matriarch's retinue of rafts. 'I was born there,' he said abruptly. 'I grew up there. It is not a pleasant place. Most of it is desert, a barren wilderness in which nothing grows. It is scarred with old wounds, littered with the ruins of bygone ages. But there is life, of a kind, and ships come to tend that life.'

'And?'

'I stowed away on such a ship. I was young, alone, more than a little desperate. I was more than lucky. The captain should have evicted me but he had a kind heart. He was old and had no son.' He paused. 'That was a long time ago. I was ten at the time.'

He shook himself as if shedding unpleasant memories. 'I've been travelling ever since. Deeper and deeper into the inhabited world. That's all there is to it, my lady. Just an ordinary story of a run-away boy who had more luck than he deserved or thought existed. But Earth is very real.'

'Then why haven't I heard of it? Why does everyone think of it as a planet that does not exist?' She stooped and picked up a handful of dirt. 'Earth! This is earth! Every planet, in a way, is earth.'

'But one planet was the original.' He saw the look of shocked realization followed immediately by forceful nega- tion. 'You do not believe me — I cannot blame you for that, but think about it for a moment. Earth, my Earth, is far from the edge of the inhabited worlds. No one now, aside from a few, has any reason to go there. But assume for a moment that what I claim is true. Men would venture from that planet in which direction? To the stars closest to home, naturally. And from there? To other, close stars. And so on until the centre of civilisation had moved deeper into the galaxy and Earth became less than a legend.' He paused. 'No, my lady, I can't blame you for not knowing of Earth. But I do.'

It made a peculiar kind of sense and held the seeds of logic. Add a few thousand years, the trials of colonial enterprise, the distorting effects of time, and what was once real becomes legend. And who, in their right senses, believes in legend? The name, of course, didn't help. And how could he identify his sun?

Seena felt a sudden wave of sympathy as she recognized his problem.

'You want to go back there.' Her eyes searched his face. 'You want to and you can't because no one seems to know where it is. That is why you told Melga of the planet of your origin — you hoped that she would be able to help you.'

'I thought that she, or someone, might know of it,' he admitted. 'I was wrong.'

'A barren place,' she murmured. 'A desert scarred with the wounds of old wars. And yet there is life there?'

'Of a kind.'

'And ships visit?'

'Yes.'

'Then you have your clues. Someone must know the coordinates. Tell me of that life, those ships.'

'No.'

'But why not?' Her eyes lightened. 'Dyne could help you. Sometimes I think he knows everything.'

'Yes,' said Dumarest tightly. 'I think you could be right.'

* ★ *

The column crawled on, two and a half miles an hour, an easy pace even for weak men loaded with half their weight in supplies. Megan grunted as he threw his weight against the rope, feeling the pull at the cuts on his shoulders, snarling in frustrated hate at the thought of the man who had plied the whip.

He still worked for the same man despite what he had promised Dumarest. There was pride in his decision and something more. The Prince had contracted to pay for his services and pay he would. Megan relished the thought of the money; the best salve of all to his scarred back.

He grunted again as a passing guard scowled at him, heaving on the rope, twisting his face into a sneer. The guard passed on. Ahead lay only darkness relieved by the ghost-light of the stars but Megan needed no light. He had been this way too often in the past. Ahead lay the mountains of Gath.

The Prince of Emmened could see them in fine detail. He peered through the infra-red binoculars clamped to his eyes then grunted with petulant irritation.

'Nothing.' He lowered the glasses. 'Just an ordinary mountain range, weathered but perfectly natural.' He slumped in his throne-like chair, ringed fingers drumming on one of the arms. 'Why?' he demanded. 'Why the sudden move? I understand that the factor had assured you that there was plenty of time.'

'He did, my lord,' said Crowder.

'Then he either lied or that old Bitch of Kund must know something. I doubt that he lied.' His face darkened. 'What is she likely to gain, Crowder?'

'Nothing, my lord. Whatever time she saved she lost while staying at the camp. Now you are in the lead. If there is anything to find you will discover it first.'

'If I knew what to look for.'

'Perhaps there is nothing, my lord.'

'That is ridiculous! She must be here for a reason. She must have left early because of that reason. Perhaps she found it at the camp and so could afford to delay. Perhaps not. It could be important. I must know what it is.'

'It could be that she merely wished to remove her ward from temptation,' soothed the courtier. Crowder was cunning in his diplomacy. 'I was watching when Moidor died,' he lied. 'You were right, my lord. She is a woman to be stirred by the sight of blood. Had there been another such bout I doubt if all the old woman's guards could have kept her from slaking her passion.'

'You think so?' The prince had known many such women.

'I know so, my lord.' Crowder was emphatic. 'And it is obvious to whom she would turn. Who else, other than yourself, could she regard as an equal?' He caught the beginning of a frown. 'Or her superior,' he hastily amended. 'Such a woman needs to be dominated. A strong hand, my lord. She has been pampered too long.'

'Perhaps.' The prince was thinking of other things. Again he lifted the binoculars and stared at the scene ahead. Again he saw only what nature had fashioned; a high ridge of weathered and fretted stone bulking huge against the stars. He swung the glasses to the west and saw only the sea and empty sky; to the east, then paused as he spotted the couple. The sight of the woman reminded him of the courtier's words; the man of the blood-bout in which he had lost his favourite.

'Crowder.'

'My lord?'

The prince handed him the glasses. 'Over there. What do you see?'

'The Lady Seena and the man Dumarest.'

'And?'

'The guards of the Matriarch.'

'They attend her at all times,' mused the prince. He was thoughtful. Crowder would have been surprised at the expression on his face but the courtier was busy with the glasses.

'Guards can be circumvented, my lord.' Crowder handed back the binoculars. 'The girl could be won.'

And, thought the prince, with her, the knowledge of the Matriarch's intentions which she must hold.

'You interest me, Crowder,' he said blandly. 'It would be intriguing to see if you were correct in your assumptions. The girl could be won, you say?'

'Yes, my lord. And, once the thing was accomplished, what could she do? She or that old woman of Kund?' Crowder smiled as the prince pondered the question.

'Assassination,' he said after a moment. 'Those guards of hers would go through hell itself if so ordered. I have no desire, Crowder, to live in constant fear of unexpected death. The suggestion displeases me.'

'But if the thing could be so arranged that she could be proven to be willing — ' Crowder was sweating but not from the heat. 'The Matriarch could hardly object to you as a husband for her ward. A monk of the Brotherhood could tie the knot.' His chuckle was a suggestive leer. 'A knot which you could cut whenever you so decided, my lord. That goes without question.'

The prince nodded, toying with the suggestion, seeing beyond the apparent simplicity of the courtier's plan. And yet it was an intriguing concept. The girl was attractive, aligned to wealth, it would be a good match. It would kill the monotony of the homeward flight if nothing else and give him the aura of responsibility the lack of which his ministers so deplored.

At the worst he could always pose as her saviour and gain her confidence via the path of blood.

Crowder's blood, naturally. The secret of Gath was worth a dozen such as he.

10

They reached the mountains, the path opening to a sickle-shaped plain which curved its narrow length between the mountains and the sea. Megan guided them to the summit of the cliffs below which the sea rolled in thunderous fury. He halted and dropped the rope.

'Here,' he announced. 'This is the best place to stay.'

One of the guards stepped closer to the edge, looked at the fury below. 'Are you sure?'

'I'm sure.' Megan's face was strained in the cold glow of the lights. 'This is the place.'

The Prince of Emmened looked down from his seat on the raft. He listened to the hungry roar of the sea and spoke to Crowder.

'Did the factor tell you which place was best?'

'No, my lord. But this man has been here many times before. He should know.'

'He should,' agreed the prince, 'but he is one we whipped on the first part of the journey. We will go closer to the mountains. Much closer.'

He leaned back, smiling in ironical amusement as Crowder gave the order, smiling still wider as he saw how Megan's shoulders flinched from the weight of the rope. It had been a brave attempt but it had failed and he could gain satisfaction from the smallest of victories.

'That man,' he told Crowder, pointing to Megan. 'When we camp give him nothing. If he argues tell him that he is paying for his failure. He will understand.'

'My lord?'

'You are a fool, Crowder,' said the prince. 'Just do as I say.'

The Matriarch of Kund had no need to make a decision. Her retinue continued to the base of the foothills, well away from the sea, her rafts covering a generous expanse of ground. Too generous in view of the limited room and the number wanting to occupy it, but she had no thought for the problems of others. As her guards set up the tents she sat and brooded in the thick, warm darkness, her mind busy with the necessity to make a decision she had put off for too long.

She didn't move as the guards surrounded her with the plastic fabric of a tent, stiffening the walls and roof with inflatable sections, joining them to others so that she sat in the centre of a growing complex of rooms. Later they would unpack some of her possessions, the tapestries, the mirror, other things. Now they were racing to beat the storm.

Dyne watched them with cerebral amusement. He knew to the minute exactly when the storm was due and knew, despite the time spent on the journey, that it was far from imminent. There was still plenty of time for him to do what had to be done.

'You will go to the mountains,' he ordered two of his personal retinue, the stern young men who accepted him as their master in all things. 'I want samples of air, ice and stone. You will take them from the mountain before, during and after the storm. I also want a continuous sampling of the air. Is that clear?'

They bowed.

'Go now and set up your equipment. Check it thoroughly. I will accept no excuse for failure. One other thing!' He called them back when they had almost reached the door. 'You will wear ear-muffs at all times. Do you understand? You will not listen to the noises of Gath. Now go.'

Alone he stepped to the door of his chamber and called to the remaining member of his retinue. 'Total seal,' he ordered. His fingers were shaking a little as he boosted the power of his bracelet.

It was intoxicating, his communion with the gestalt of the Cyclan, and strong mental discipline was necessary to ration the use of the Samatchazi formulae, the activating of the Homochon elements. A discipline which if not strong enough would be enforced from without. But he had reason for contact. He had nothing to fear and much to anticipate.

His own reward could scarcely be less than immediate acceptance to the community of brains resting in the depths of their lonely world.

The narrow plain was alive with men, tents, guards, tourists and travellers. They were scattered thick on the crescent of land between the mountains and the sea, the glow of their lights and the red eyes of their fires a mosaic of living colour in the sullen weight of the air.

'Those fires,' said Seena. 'When the wind blows won't they be dangerous?'

'With the storm will come rain,' said Dumarest. He had learned as much from Megan. 'Even if it didn't the flames wouldn't last long. There is nothing to burn aside from the grass.' And the clothing of the travellers and some of the tourists, he thought, but didn't mention it. They were fools to have fires at such a time in such a place, but men have always yearned for the comfort of a dancing flame.

'It's eerie,' she said, and shivered slightly, but not from the cold. 'It's as if something were about to happen at any moment.'

'The storm,' he said absently. His eyes

ranged from the stunted bulk of the mountains to where the plain fell into the sea. At one time the plain must have been much wider, the mountains much higher. The ocean and the wind had eaten at them both. Soon there would be no plain at all and only the sullen waves would hear the lauded music of the spheres. He mentioned it and she shrugged.

'If there is really such a thing. It seems hard to believe.'

'So?' He was curious. 'Why else did you come to Gath?'

'I attend the Matriarch.'

'And she?'

'Goes where she will.' He recognized the tone, he had heard it from the physician, a reminder of their relative positions. 'I do not question the Matriarch,' she said pointedly.

'And I should not?' He was unimpressed. 'Why are you here, my lady? To listen to the sound of dead voices? To stand with your face to the wind and hear the dirge of a dying world? These things are for tourists.'

'I am the ward of the Matriarch!'

'Yes,' he said softly. 'And she is old and has not yet, so I understand, named her successor. Would that be you, my lady? Are you destined to be the next Matriarch of Kund?'

'You forget yourself!' She was rigid with anger. 'What would you, a traveller, know of such things?'

'Are you, my lady?'

He was on dangerous ground, more dangerous than he'd thought. A shadow grew from the gloom and thickened into the face and form of the captain of the Matriarch's guard. Elspeth was coldly polite.

'You are needed, my lady,' she said to the girl. 'You are not,' she snapped at Dumarest. 'Come, my lady.'

He watched them go then wandered slowly through the camp. He spotted where Sime had planted his coffin and himself, hugging the perimeter of the Matriarch's tented area. The old crone, some way off, busied herself over a fire. The dancing light made her look like a witch. She didn't look up as he passed.

Dumarest continued on his way. He

was looking for Megan.

He halted as someone touched his arm, recognizing one of the monks by the light of a nearby fire.

'Yes?'

'Your name is Dumarest?'

'That's right. You want me?'

'A friend of yours has been hurt. He asked for you.' The monk turned to lead the way. 'If you will follow me, brother?'

★　★　★

Megan lay prone on a couch of uprooted grass gathered in one corner of the portable church. He wore no shirt and his back was marked with long, livid welts. They had not been caused by a normal whip. Dumarest knelt to examine them. His face was hard as he stared at the monk in attendance.

'When?'

'We found him a short while ago close to the edge of the cliffs. He was scarcely conscious. He asked for you.' Brother Angelo tenderly applied salve to the welts. Dumarest knocked aside his hand.

162

'That stuff is useless. He's been beaten with a strag. He needs sedatives and neutralizers.'

'I know, brother.' The man was very calm. 'But we can only use what we have.'

It wasn't enough. The dried, flexible body of a sea-serpent found in the oceans of Strag carried a searingly painful nerve-poison in its jagged scales. Its use was much favoured by overseers and the aristocracy for the punishment of slaves and underlings. Dumarest felt his muscles knot with rage as he looked at the thin shoulders and fleshless back of his friend.

'Go to the tents of the Matriarch,' he said. 'She is not unsympathetic. Buy what you need.' He searched his pockets for the bonus-money he had won. He spilled it all into the monk's hands. 'Hurry!'

Gently he stooped over the moaning figure. A cold hand gripped his stomach as he exposed the face. A lash across the eyes with a strag brought permanent blindness. Megan had been lucky. The lash which had marked his cheeks had missed his eyes. The welts on the back of his hands showed why.

'What happened?' Dumarest leaned close to the other's mouth. 'Who did this?'

'Crowder.' The voice was a tormented whisper. 'The prince refused to pay me — said that it was the price of failure. Crowder added to the price.' A spasm contorted the sweating features. 'God! The pain!'

'Steady!' Dumarest gripped the thin shoulder. 'Why did he refuse to pay you?'

'I tried to be smart.' Megan sobbed in his agony. 'Stay away from the cliffs, Earl. When the wind blows sometimes people get the urge to run. Sometimes they run right over the edge. I've seen them do it.'

'So?'

'I tried to get the prince to camp close to the edge of the cliff. I thought that, when the wind blew, he might go over. Teach the swine a lesson . . . whips his . . . ' The mumbling voice rose to a scream. 'The pain! God, the pain!'

'Is there nothing you can do!' Dumarest glared up at the remaining monk. Brother Benedict spread his hands, his face sympathetic in the glow of the single lamp.

'Strag poison lowers the pain level so that a scratch becomes almost unendurable agony. Until the poison has been neutralized or dissipated that condition will remain.'

'I know that.' Dumarest was impatient. 'What of your hypnotic techniques?' He snarled as the monk made no answer. 'Damn it, I know about your benediction-light. This man went to church back at the field. He must still be prone to your suggestions. Work on him, damn it!'

'Easy, brother.' The monk was gentle but firm. 'We have already tried that. Hypnosis requires the co-operation of the subject. Strag poison makes that impossible.' He paused. 'We do not like to see the effects of pain, brother,' he continued gently. 'There is too much suffering in the universe for us to wish for more.'

'I believe you.' Dumarest hesitated. Humanity all belonged to the same root but there were many branches. What would be harmless to one could be serious injury to another. Then Megan screamed and decided the matter.

'Steady,' soothed Dumarest. 'Steady.'

He rested his hands on Megan's throat, his thumbs probing the flesh. He sought and found the carotids then pressed, cutting off the blood supply to the brain. Brother Benedict stepped forward, his face anxious.

'Be careful, brother!'

Dumarest nodded, counting the seconds. A little pressure should bring unconsciousness, too much would result in death. But he was unsure of the exact effect of strag poison on the body's metabolism. Even less sure of what mutational divergencies Megan might carry in his body. It would take so little, a slight alteration in the oxygen-needs of the brain, a lowering of the reviving effect of fresh blood. Even an unsuspected weakness . . .

He removed his hands.

Megan screamed.

'I tried that, brother.' The monk was quick to lessen his failure. 'That and pressure on certain nerves of the spine. We can do nothing, the poison has beaten us. Perhaps Brother Angelo will have better success.'

They didn't have long to wait. Dumarest

sprang to his feet as the monk returned from his errand. He was empty-handed.

'I am sorry, brother.' He handed back the money. 'The Matriarch has sealed her area.'

'Sealed?' Dumarest fought his anger. 'Did you see the physician? The Lady Seena?'

'No one, brother.'

'Damn it! Did you try?'

'I tried,' said the monk with dignity. 'But I could not get past the guards.'

Dumarest winced as Megan began to moan.

★ ★ ★

The guard was a vague shadow against the bulk of the tent. He snapped up his weapon, his voice hard.

'Halt!'

Dumarest halted, then moved slowly forward. 'I want to see your master.'

'Who are you?'

'Dumarest. I killed his fighter.'

'I saw it.' The guard became more friendly. He lowered his weapon together with his voice. 'A nice bout. It was about time that pimp got what was coming to him but you were too gentle. Your footwork was fine but you took a chance at the end. You should have — '

'I won,' snapped Dumarest impatiently. 'Are you going to announce me?'

'Well — ' The guard was doubtful. 'What is your business with the prince?'

'Personal. Now call his flunky and tell him that I want to see his master. Move!'

It was a gamble but he had nothing to lose. If the guard did his duty he would refuse even to announce the visitor but Dumarest was banking both on his reputation and the factor of curiosity. It was a gamble he won.

'What is this?' Crowder came from the tent, his face puffed in the light of a torch he held above his head. A thin, glistening tube almost a foot in length dangled from a chain about his right wrist. Dumarest knew what it contained. 'What is it you want? Your prize? That is with the factor. What else?'

'I will tell that to the prince.'

Crowder flushed and dropped his right

hand, catching the tube and fingering the catch. A slight pressure and the strag would spring from its sheath. One slash and the man would have reason to regret his insolence. Then he hesitated, remembering where he had last seen Dumarest, and with whom. A man so friendly with the Lady Seena could have his uses. He let the tube slip from his hand.

'You must tell it to me,' he said mildly. 'The prince cannot be bothered without good reason.'

'I want drugs,' said Dumarest harshly. Crowder had been the pressure of a finger away from death. 'Is that reason enough?'

'Of course.' The courtier smiled. 'Come with me.'

The prince was at play when they entered his chamber. He sat staring at the focused image of a solidiograph, his eyes glazed as he studied the variations of an age-old theme, entranced by the depicted skill. Not until the ephemeral images had faded did Crowder urge Dumarest forward. He placed him on a selected spot before a throne-like chair and hurried to his master's side.

Dumarest failed to catch his whisperings.

He looked around, noting the luxurious hangings, the subtle air of decadence, the expected appurtenances of a Sybarite. He could see no guards but guessed at their presence. The prince was not a man to trust himself with a stranger.

'So.' He had deigned to notice his presence. 'You wanted to see me. Why?'

'For drugs, my lord.'

'So Crowder tells me. At least you are honest. Have you been addicted long?'

Dumarest restrained his impatience. Let the fool have his fun. 'The drugs are for a friend of mine,' he explained. 'A man your courtier there lashed to the brink of insanity with his strag. Was that by your order, my lord?'

'The man had displeased me. I ordered him to be punished.'

'With a strag?'

'No.'

'So I thought. Will you give me leave to punish the one responsible, my lord?'

'Crowder? Perhaps.' The prince was amused. His full lips parted to show

170

gleaming white teeth as he smiled. He considered himself to be an attractive man. Physically he was. 'You are a brave man,' he mused. 'Are you willing to risk your life for a friend?'

'If necessary. He could have saved mine.'

'And you are grateful.' The prince was pleased with the answer. 'Tell me,' he said gently. 'What will you give me if I do as you ask?'

'Ten times the cost of the drugs, my lord,' said Dumarest promptly.

The prince shook his head.

'The High passage I won by defeating your fighter.'

'So much?'

'If necessary, my lord. A man is in pain.'

'And you want the cure for his agony.' The prince gestured to Crowder. 'Find my physician. Have him give you what is needed. Go!' He waited until the man had left. 'Come closer,' he ordered Dumarest. 'Closer. That is better.' He leaned forward and lowered his voice. 'You see? I trust you. I have placed myself within your power.'

'Have you, my lord?'

The prince caught the irony. 'You are wise. Only a fool would wholly trust another. You are no fool and neither am I. There is a thing you could do for me. If you agree I will give you the drugs and the cost of a High passage.' He paused. 'The drugs now, the passage later. You could use it for your friend.'

Dumarest nodded, waiting.

'I have seen you close to the Lady Seena,' continued the prince. 'She is an attractive woman. I would like to know her better. You understand?'

'Yes, my lord.'

'Good. What I ask is simple. It could be that I shall need a friend who is close to the lady in question. You could be that friend. If so you must obey my orders without question or hesitation. You agree?'

'Certainly, my lord.' Dumarest hesitated. 'The High passage?'

'Comes when your work is done.' The prince lifted his hand for silence as Crowder entered. The courtier carried a small package.

'The drugs, my lord.'

'Give them to Dumarest and escort him from the area.'

The prince was thoughtful as the men left the room. He felt a vague sense of unease, Dumarest had been too willing to agree, then he shrugged off the feeling. How could he compare the values of a common traveller with those of a cultured man? Dumarest had nothing, to him the Lady Seena was a woman as distant as the stars while the price of a High passage was something which he could appreciate. No, he had reacted according to his type and would prove a useful tool when the time came to act.

The prince smiled as he thought about it. Crowder had done better than he knew.

Outside the tent Dumarest wiped the sweat from his palms and tucked the package under his arm. He felt dirty, soiled, yet there had been nothing else he could have done. Megan needed the drugs and, if he had to lie to get them, so what?

He frowned as he walked to where the

monks waited in the shelter of their tiny church. It was hard to see, thick cloud had rolled from the east and covered the sky, blotting out the stars. They made the air even more oppressive, a lid clamped down on the oven below, stifling with their presence.

Dumarest didn't look at the sky. He was thinking about the Lady Seena and the Prince of Emmened. What did they have in common? What plan had the prince in mind and what would be his part in it?

Something hit wetly on the back of his hand. Another drop followed it, another until, in seconds, the air was heavy with falling rain. At the same time a vivid flash of lightning ripped across the sky.

The storm had begun.

11

It came with a continuous rolling of thunder which tore at the ears and numbed the senses. The lightning was a web of electric fire across the sky, stabbing at the ground, searing wetly into the sea. The rain was a deluge, pounding the ground into mud, turning the air almost solid with its moisture.

The fires died. Stretched plastic echoed the drumbeat of the rain. Tourists cursed and huddled beneath the shelter of their rafts. Travellers fought to join them or scurried frantically to what shelter they could find. It was little. The wise stripped their shirts and covered their heads so that, at least, they could breathe. The stupid drowned in the relentless downpour.

And still the air remained motionless. The winds had yet to come.

'I don't like it,' said Megan. He sat, hunched in a corner of the church, his face pale from recent strain. 'I've never known it this bad before.'

'But it rains?'

'Sure.' Megan moved so as to give Dumarest a little more room. The church was crowded with desperate travellers sheltering from the storm. They stood packed in an almost solid mass. The air was heavy with their heat and smell after their long confinement. 'It rains and sometimes there's thunder but not to this extent.' He listened to the drumming of the rain. 'This is something special.'

He was shouting but Dumarest could hardly hear what he said. The thunder and rain seemed to fill the universe. Suddenly he could no longer stand the cramped confinement, the heat and the smell.

'I'm going outside.' He tried to rise to his feet and Megan caught his arm.

'Wait it out, Earl. You're safe in here.'

Safety was relative. In the church Dumarest was safe from the immediate danger of the rain but the rain would not last forever. Then would come fresh danger, perhaps from the Prince of

Emmened, or Crowder, or the person who had tried to kill him on the journey. The violence of the storm triggered a violence within so that he burned with the need for action.

He jerked free his arm and tried to thrust his way towards the opening of the church. He failed. The press of men was too great. He dropped to his knees and probed the lower part of the wall. The plastic was thin, merging with the sea of mud outside. He dug and lifted and gasped as spattered rain lashed his face.

'Earl!'

'Wait here!'

Dumarest lifted the side wall, ignoring Megan's protest, flattening so that he could thrust head and shoulders outside. The rain slammed at his skull and forced it into the mud. He reached out and clawed at the ground, dragging the rest of his body from the tent. The side wall fell behind him and, suddenly, he was alone.

Alone in a peculiar world lit by the stroboscopic effect of vivid flashes of lightning, deafening with the roll of thunder, the drumming of rain.

He turned and felt water drive into his nostrils, his mouth, slam with bruising force against his closed eyelids, run wetly into his ears. He tried to breathe and choked as water reached his lungs. Coughing, he turned to face the mud, stooping low as he ran forward in a long, loping crouch.

He paused to get his bearings, conscious of the proximity of the sea and the cliffs falling to the waves. In such a storm it would be easy to go over the edge. A lightning flash showed him his position. Ahead and to one side loomed the tents of the Matriarch, black in the fierce glare. He could see no guards but had expected none. They would be inside. Another flash and he could see the complex of the Prince of Emmened, equally black, equally lifeless. The rafts of the tourists rested, well away from the sea, a cluster of crowded misery. Small mounds lay scattered between, huddled travellers devoid of shelter, some alive, some dead, all inconspicuous in the mud.

He ran forward as darkness closed around.

It was hard work, harder still as he had to steal every breath, shielding his face and waiting as his gasping lungs re-oxygenated his blood, retching as water reached where only air should go. Waiting too as the vivid glare of lightning etched the plain with stark clarity, running only when it was safe to move unobserved.

The rain eased a little. The rolling thunder moved seawards, the lightning was no longer directly overhead.

Dumarest tripped and fell, slamming heavily into the mud, feeling the soft dirt splash into his eyes and mouth. He rolled, face upwards, so that the punishing rain could wash him clean, rolling again in order to breathe. He looked at what had tripped him.

He looked thoughtfully at a boy, scarcely a man, the one who had travelled with Sime and the crone. He was quite dead.

Drowned, perhaps, caught in the storm and not knowing what to do in order to survive. He lay face-upwards, his face very pale beneath the patina of rain, his thin hands crossed on his stomach, his lips parted, his hair a dark smear on his forehead. Dumarest reached out and turned his head, waiting for a flash of lightning before turning it to the other side.

The sky crackled with a livid glare and he saw, quite clearly, the little red spot high on the cheek, just before the ear and below the temple.

A spot which could have been made by the thrust of a heavy needle.

The rain ceased. The thunder muttered into silence. The lightning blazed on the horizon in a lambent chiaroscuro. Far to the west the libration of the planet thrust a wall of cold air into the tropic heat of the sun. The thermodynamic balance began to change. Equally far to the east a cold bank of frigid air began to move, drawn by the vacuum of expansion. It speeded as it moved, rushing over the cold of the nightside towards the warmth of the sun. It swept across the plains of ice and hummocks of frost and streamed down on the mountains. It hit and surrounded the obstruction, blowing up and over, forcing its way through cracks and crevasses, bathing the fretted and filigreed mass of stone and crystal with the thrust of its passage.

The air became murmurous with sound.

Ghost sound. The distant skirl of pipes, the crying wail of strings, the heartbeat of rattling drums, all mingled and faint, thin and unimpressive.

The wind blew stronger.

And the dead rose to talk again.

Dumarest rose from where he knelt beside the body. Around him streamed a medley of voices, a cacophony of sound, a vibration which covered the audible range and extended far beyond. He heard his name and turned and saw nothing. He caught the echo of a laugh, the snarl of a curse, the thin tremolo of a baby's wail. He closed his eyes.

Immediately the sounds grew louder. A multi-toned murmur whispered past his ears and, buried within it, a voice scratched with boneless fingers at the doors of memory.

'It's your turn next, Earl. Make it doubles — I want to celebrate.'

'Carson!'

'*Don't be a fool, Earl. Why don't you settle down now that you've got the chance? Take my advice and do it before it's too late.*'

'Carson!' Dumarest opened his eyes, almost expecting to see the familiar shape of the man who had travelled with him to a dozen worlds. Carson who had gambled against the odds once too often and was now five years dead.

There was nothing. Only the mountains, the wind, the thin wavering of the unmistakable voice. That and the cries of the others, the travellers and tourists, who had left their shelter to stand, entranced, exposed to the magic of the winds of Gath.

Again he closed his eyes, the illusion was better that way, more complete. Now the voices were clear and strong ringing from the winds which blew about his head. Many voices, some of men who had tried to kill him, others of men he had killed. Moidor sneered his challenge, Benson murmured his envy, he heard the spiteful whine of a phygria, the hot snarl of a laser. The past unfolded and the dead became real.

The old captain who had taken pity on a scared and frightened boy.

'*One thing, son. You must promise never to tell anyone of this. Never mention it or go into detail. If you do it will cost my life. Do you understand?*'

The promise he had kept until now and then only broken in part. But a man should know how to find his home.

Other voices, harsh, impatient, some appealing. A dizzying blend of sound containing within itself all the voices he had ever heard, all the promises and threats he had ever known. And one voice, warm with sensuous passion, whispering with rising emotion, tearing at his heart with painful memory . . . '*Darling . . . darling . . . darling . . .* '

'No!'

He jerked open his eyes. The past was dead, she was dead, let it lie. But the temptation was strong. To hear her again, to thrill to her words of love, to recapture the joy of the past and warm his spirit in tender memory . . .

Savagely he shook his head. The voice was a lure, an illusion without flesh or real meaning, a ghost from the past born in his own head from memories impossible to eradicate. Now he could understand Megan's warning. How many had run to their death thinking that they ran to the arms of their lovers, family, friends?

Or ran from some imagined danger which tore at their sanity.

He gritted his teeth against the rising wind. Around him the plain was in turmoil. Men sat entranced, beating time to invisible orchestras, walking as if in a dream, standing with tears running down their faces or cursing or holding conversations with the empty air. They stood revealed in the flicker of the distant lightning. Helpless in the grip of their illusions.

The wind blew stronger.

★ ★ ★

High on the mountain a young man checked his instruments and felt the rising force of the wind. He heard nothing, the muffs clamped to his ears deadened all sound, but he was curious. The instruments required little attention and it was doubtful if he would ever again visit Gath. And, if he should listen, just for a short while, who would ever know?

He lifted his muffs and listened and screamed and fell two hundred feet to his death.

On the plain the Prince of Emmened blanched as voices rang in his head, sharp, accusing, the words of men long dead, the sobs of women long forgotten. He cried out and the physician came running, an old man, long deaf, the electrodes of his mechanical ears glistening against the hairless dome of his skull.

'The voices!' screamed the prince. 'The voices!'

The physician read his lips. He had turned off the power for his ears when the wind had first brought its pleasure and pain and he could guess at what troubled his master.

'Think of pleasant things,' he suggested. 'Of the sighs of women, the laughter of children, the song of the birds.'

'Fool!' The prince snarled his anger but the man made sense. More sense than the wind which carried the tormenting voices. But he could not do it alone. 'Bring drugs,' he ordered. 'Euphorics. Hurry!'

Drugged, dreamlike, drifting in illusion, the prince sprawled in his chair and thought of pleasant things. Of combats and diversions yet to come. Of the richness which life had to offer and the painful joy of complex jests. Painful to the victims, of course, never to him. And he thought of the Lady Seena, the most pleasant thing of all.

He was not alone. Rigid in her chair, her room open to the air, the Matriarch of Kund sat alone in a world of memories. She listened again to the deep, strong voice of a man and could imagine his touch, firm yet tender, the hands on her shoulders, her waist, the curve of her hips. Her lips pursed to his kiss, the blood running hot in her aged veins.

'Darling!' she whispered. 'Oh, my darling!'

'*My love*,' echoed the voice in her

mind. *'Gloria, my love. I am yours for all eternity. We are meant to be together — I cannot live without you. My darling, my love, my own!'*

A man, dust for over eighty years, now talking and breathing at her side, his voice, his beloved voice, soft in her ears.

'I love you, my darling. I love you . . . love you . . . love you . . . '

Another voice, thin, high, childish.

'Mummy! Look, mummy. See what I have!'

A scrap of root shaped in the likeness of a man. A doll drawn from nature. Arms and legs and the rudiments of a face. With cosmetics she had drawn in the details, the eyes and lips and ears. With lace from her handkerchief she had fashioned a dress. The sun had been warm, that day, and the air full of tenderness. Her heart ached with the memory of it.

And other voices, the thin, whispering echoes of ambition, the temptation of office and the knowledge that the coveted prize was hers — for a price.

'Mummy,' whispered the voice, the

thin, girlish voice. '*When am I going to see you again?*'

The tears ran unheeded down her withered cheeks.

Dyne crouched over his recorder, his head grotesque under the muffs which covered his ears, his eyes burning with the light of scientific dedication. Around him the wind moaned against the tents, the drumming of the plastic adding to the medley, re-enforcing rather than blanketing the catholic noise.

On the machine the tapes wound soundlessly from their spools, recording every note of the entire spectrum of audible sound, recording even the sub- and ultra-sonic vibrations beyond the range of normal hearing. It was a sensitive instrument. It would miss nothing but it would solve nothing. It lacked the catalyst of the brain which could transmute sound into imaginary image.

The cyber leaned back, pensive, wondering at the world of emotion of which he knew nothing. The secret of Gath was, to him, no secret. It was merely a combination of circumstances which had a cumulative effect. The mighty sounding-board of the mountains which, beneath the thrust of the wind, responded in terms of living sound. Sound which could trigger thought-associations so that the hearer would live in a world of temporary hallucination. Sound which could be filtered by the brain to form actual words, music, songs and declamations.

Sound which contained within itself the sum total of every noise that had been made or could be made in the lifetime of the universe.

That was the unique attraction of Gath.

He shifted, a little restlessly, conscious of the sound without actually being able to hear it. Coldly his mind evaluated the incident. There was nothing mysterious about it. There were only so many cycles to the range of the human ear. There were only so many combinations of sound possible within that range. Given enough time, each of those combinations must be played.

He made a slight adjustment to the recorder.

Dumarest gritted his teeth and clamped his hands over his ears. It made little difference. The blast of the wind was not so easily beaten, the voices refused to be silenced.

He felt that he stood in the centre of a shouting crowd, all yelling against the thunder of music, the accumulated roar of factories. He heard the hissing whine of rocket engines, the rolling crescendo of atomic destruction, the thudding blast of endless cannon. He heard the screams of burning men, the shrieks of ravaged women. The wail of tormented children made a threnody of pain laced with hymns, paeans, the shanties of drunken seamen. The creak of ropes blended with the sullen throb of engines.

'No!'

His shout was lost in the wind. The storm was too strong, the wind too powerful, human resistance too low.

Lightning cast its garish light over the plain. He could see a musician beating time, his eyes glazed with madness. A tourist ran recklessly towards the sea. A traveller ripped at his clothes, his nails raking his flesh. Voices drummed within his skull.

'Blessed are the meek for they shall inherit . . . '

'E equals MC squared . . . '

'The Curfew tolls the knell of parting . . . '

'No, Harry! For God's sake . . . '

'Two drops and . . . '

A million voices in a thousand tongues merging with the natural sounds, the factory noises, the music and songs and sounds of peace and war so that they, like the mingled colours of the spectrum, formed a 'white,' composite noise.

Dumarest groaned with the pain of his ears.

Rational thought was impossible. It was hard to concentrate, words formed themselves to follow the trend of thought, mental images flocked to dull logical sequence.

He stooped and grabbed handfuls of wet dirt. He lifted the mud and slammed it over his ears, piling it high, adding to the sticky stuff until the impact of the wind had fallen to a low murmur. The dead man watched him from where he lay.

Waiting for Dumarest to join him in the mud.

He turned barely in time, catching a glimpse of naked metal, the afterglow of a lightning flash on polished steel. He jerked sideways, his skin crawling to the fear of poison. A small shape hit him as he grabbed at the wrist. He missed and doubled as a foot drove into his groin. Half-blinded with pain he backed and fell over the body of the dead man.

The glare of lightning showed him the figure of the crone, eyes wild, ears muffled, the heavy needle poised over his eyes.

He grabbed, rolling as the light died, managing to wrench the sliver of steel from her hand. The mud fell from his ears and his head ached to the wind-borne hammer of sound. He felt a lithe body, gripped it, hands searching for the throat. He missed, felt metal instead and ripped the muffs from her ears.

And lost her in the darkness.

He sprang to his feet as the next flash lit the sky. He saw her running away from him, heading towards the cliffs and the sea below. He followed, slipping in the mud, retching from the pain in his groin. He saw her once more, a ragged figure silhouetted against the sky, then she vanished as the light died.

She was gone when the next flash came.

Slowly Dumarest walked back towards the mountains. He scooped up fresh mud to cover his ears, wondering how long the storm would last, how intense it would grow. The limit must be very close. Sheer sound, alone, could not kill but the accompanying ultra-sonics could. If there were ultra-sonics. From the pain in his ears he knew that the possibility was high.

He reached the dead man, passed him, continued towards the tents of the Matriarch. He was close to the area, heading to where Sime had rested his coffin, when the storm reached its climax.

The wind fell. The lightning flared raggedly in the sky and nature seemed to hold its breath. Things took on a peculiar clarity in the electric illumination, somehow unreal caught as they were in the stroboscopic effect of the lightning.

Then, as if it had merely paused to gather strength, the wind returned in a savage gust which surpassed all that had gone before.

And, in the eerie flicker of the lightning, Dumarest saw the lid of Sime's coffin rise, tilting, falling aside from the rising figure below.

12

Dumarest groaned and opened his eyes. He looked at a clear sky dotted with stars, the pale crescents of two moons close to the horizon. He was cold, shivering, his head throbbing to a dull, monotonous ache. He lifted a hand and felt his temple. It was swollen and sticky with congealed blood. He winced as he pressed the wound, feeling relief in the discovery that it was only superficial.

A shape stooped over him, the face suddenly springing to life in the light of a torch held to one side, fading as it was carried further away. Megan stooped lower, his breathing rapid, hands reaching to touch Dumarest in the region of the heart. They halted as he caught the gleam of open eyes.

'What happened?'

'The rafts tore free from their moorings,' said Megan quickly. 'One of them must have hit you. I tripped over you and thought you might be dead.' He looked pale, his face ghastly in the thin light. 'There was a dead man lying close to where I found you.'

'I know.'

'There's a lot of dead.' Megan leaned forward to help as Dumarest sat upright. 'Too many dead, tourists as well as travellers.' He shuddered. 'God! What a storm! I've never seen one like it and hope never to see it again.'

He shuddered again, pulling sodden rags tight across his chest. The air was frigid with nightside chill and the ground felt crusty as if coated with ice. Dumarest rose to his feet and looked around.

The place resembled a battlefield. Only the tents of the Matriarch and those of the Prince of Emmened had withstood the final gusts. The rafts had been blown out to sea. The remains of the church lay a tatter of plastic on the ground. The two monks moved from figure to figure, their torches centring them in pools of light, narrowing as they knelt. Sometimes they called for others to help them move a man in whom they had found life. They did not call often.

'The ultra-sonics,' said Megan quietly. 'They didn't know enough to take care of themselves — or were too far gone to care.' He scratched at the sides of his head and caked mud fell from the region of his ears. His teeth chattered from the biting cold.

'We need shelter and warmth,' said Dumarest. He looked at the tents of the Matriarch, they blazed with light and seemed ringed with guards. He looked towards those of the prince. The lights were few, the guards invisible. 'Get the men and follow me.'

'To the tents of the prince?' Megan blanched with recent memory. 'He's not going to like that.'

'I don't care what he likes. If those men want to freeze they can stay here. If not they'd better follow.'

The tents seemed deserted. Dumarest slowed as he approached, half-expecting the challenge of a guard, the searing blast of a laser. But nothing happened, no one stirred, no one snapped an order. He reached the tents and cautiously pressed open the vent of the outer vestibule. He stepped inside. A solitary torch glowed from a bracket. The place was empty.

He found Crowder in the second room.

The man sprawled on the carpet, naked to the waist, his upper body covered with the welts of the strag hanging from its tube in his right hand. Blood showed at his ears, his nose, seeped from the corners of his staring eyes. His jaws were clenched, the lips withdrawn so that, even in death, he snarled like a dog. The nails of his left hand were buried deep in his palm.

Dumarest stepped over him, wondering what illusion had driven him to such extremes of self-punishment, what guilt the man must have harboured. Guilt or self-contempt. Or perhaps the inaudible vibrations bathing the area had sent him insanely to his death. He would not have been alone.

A guard was slumped at the entrance to the inner chamber. He too was dead. Another whimpered in a corner, shrieking as Dumarest approached, running past him into the dark, the cold, the hungry sea. In the throne-like chair an old man smiled a greeting.

'You are Dumarest,' he said. 'I have seen you before — when you killed Moidor.'

'So?'

'I am Elgar, physician to the Prince of Emmened.' He bowed, light gleaming from his naked scalp, the electrodes of his mechanical ears. 'You do not find us at our best. This camping site was unfortunately chosen. It appears to have been at the focal point of harmful vibrations — as you perhaps have seen.'

Dumarest nodded.

'They did not switch off their ears, you see,' said Elgar seriously. 'Not as I took the precaution of doing.' Then, abruptly. 'You have a question?'

'Where is the prince?'

'Gone. Another?'

'Where has he gone?'

'Somewhere. Another?'

The man was either tottering on the edge of insanity or had a warped sense of humour. Then Dumarest saw his eyes and knew there could be a third reason. The physician was loyal to his master.

'There are men outside who will die unless they get food and warmth,' he said. 'I had hoped the prince would supply their needs.'

'He will.'

'But if he is not here?'

'You do not look like a man to be halted by such a flimsy barrier,' said the old man shrewdly. 'But force will not be necessary.'

'Have I threatened the use of force?' Dumarest wished the man would stop playing games. His head throbbed and nausea filled his stomach. He needed food, a hot bath, medicines and massage.

'No,' admitted Elgar. 'But I think that, if it came to it, not even the prince would be able to resist your demands — not without the help of his guards.' His smile grew wider. 'But this talk is foolish. I am in command. Bring the men inside. Let the monks of the Brotherhood attend to their needs. They shall have food and warmth to the full extent of my power.'

And clothes from the dead, thought Dumarest grimly, and loot from the bodies of those tourists who had no reason to object. This would be a rich occasion for the travellers who had been fortunate enough to survive.

★ ★ ★

The tapes spun on their spools, slowing to a stop, clicking as the loaded cartridges lifted from their pivots, sealing themselves in adamantine plastic for travel and storage. Dyne watched the completion of the operation. He liked the relentless efficiency of machines, the smooth workings of robotic devices. They were safe and predictable and could be of valued employment. It was a pity that men were not like machines.

He lifted the containers and packed them into a small container blazoned with the Cyclan seal. Later he would study them, break down their pattern of accumulated sound, run them through computers fitted with selector devices. It would take years, a lifetime even, but he would find all they had to give. And, if he did not, then others would. The

Cyclan had continuity.

He rose and swept aside a curtain, staring at the plain beyond the double-wall of the window, automatically checking the instruments which lined the sill. The wind had fallen almost to zero. The humidity was low, the electric-potential the same, the temperature as expected. A glance at the chronometer confirmed a previous estimate. The storm had lasted longer than usual; far longer than others would have thought. He had predicted its duration to the minute.

The knowledge gave him pleasure.

'Master.'

He turned. One of his personal retinue stood at the entrance of the room. He looked pale, strained, his eyes ringed with circles of fatigue. Dyne recognized him as one of the two he had sent to the mountains to gather data.

'Report.'

'The air samples were taken as ordered, master.' The youth moved into the room. 'The samples of rock from the mountain — ' He hesitated. Novitiates of the Cyclan were not expected to be wholly

202

devoid of emotion but they were expected never to display it. He drew a deep breath. 'The one responsible failed in his task. He fell to his death. I could not regain the samples attached to his body.'

'Do you know why he failed?'

'No, master.'

'But surely you are able to arrive at a conclusion based on known data?' The cyber's voice never altered from its soft, smooth modulation but it brought no comfort. The Cyclan had no time for failure of any kind and Dyne less than most.

'I conclude that he lifted his muffs so as to listen to the wind,' said the youth in a rush. 'I did not hear him fall. I found him only after our task was accomplished.'

'After *your* task was accomplished,' corrected Dyne. He stood, thinking. The samples of rock were of little importance — it had been worth their loss to discover a flaw in a member of his retinue. The youth was better dead. The air samples were safe and of the greater interest. If hallucogenic gases or particles had been carried by the wind they would show it. 'Give me the tapes,' he ordered. Then,

'You may go. Get food and rest.'

'Master.'

The youth bowed and left the room. Dyne locked the air sample-tapes with the others, snapping shut the case, spinning the combination lock. A flicker of light from beyond the window caught his eye. Outside scattered men with torches moved slowly in the range of his vision. He studied them, assessed them, dismissed them as of being of little importance.

He drew the curtain and stood, head tilted a little, listening. He heard nothing, the walls of his room were too thick. He crossed to the entrance and drew aside the barrier. Now he could hear it, very faint but clearly audible. The soft tinkle of laughter, the murmur of voices, the thin, unmistakable tones of the old woman. A guard walked past. He halted her with a gesture.

'Where is the Lady Thoth?'

'With the Matriarch.' The woman was polite but curt. She had little time for anyone other than her captain and her ruler. She frowned her impatience at his next question.

'Have you seen her?'

'I have.'

'Recently?'

'I have just left the chamber of the Matriarch. They are together.'

'I see.' He thanked her with his mechanical smile. 'That will be all.'

The chamber was small, bright with tapestries, heavy with the scent of spice. A glowing lamp threw soft light over the occupants. Gloria smiled as he entered.

'Dyne. You anticipate me. I was about to send for you.'

Dyne looked closely at the couple. The old woman was glowing with happiness. Sitting beside her, very close, the girl reflected some of that joy. The soft light warmed her ebon hair, the white velvet of her skin. Her lips were full and very red. Her eyes very bright. They met those of the cyber.

'The Matriarch is pleased with you,' she said. 'Because of your orders none have suffered so much as a burst eardrum.' She laughed. 'But at one time I thought that I should never hear again.'

'The storm was unusual in its violence,

my lady.' The cyber turned to the old woman. 'I came to report that the storm is over. There may be occasional gusts but the main force of the wind is spent. We are ready to depart.'

'Must we?'

'It would be best not to linger, my lady. The external temperature is low and will fall lower. Delay will make our return more arduous and there seems little need for us to extend our stay.'

She knew that well enough but, for her, Gath held magic.

'I am reluctant to leave this place,' she said slowly. 'It has wakened many memories. For a time I was young again and — ' She swallowed. 'Occasional gusts, did you say?'

'Yes, my lady.'

'Then we will stay,' she decided. 'Stay for just one of those gusts.'

For one more contact with the dead she had loved. One more brief revival of the time when she had been young and filled with the hunger of living. He recognized the lure, assessed it, realized both its futility and strength.

'Here,' said Megan. He raised his torch even higher, widening the pool of light in which they stood. 'This is where I found you.'

'You're sure?' Dumarest frowned as he tried to orient himself. In the dark all places looked the same, only the tents of the Matriarch looked familiar.

'I'm sure.' Megan was warm in his salvaged clothing, a ring with a peculiar device shone on one finger. Dumarest had seen it before. The rosily fat man would never need it again. He had made his last gamble. 'The young fellow was over there.' The torch dipped as he gestured. 'You were here.'

Dumarest nodded, dropping to one knee, his eyes narrowed as he peered into the darkness. The glimpse had been brief and the blow on the head had jarred his memory but he was sure as to what he had seen. The lid of Sime's coffin rising from pressure beneath.

His dead wife rising at the sound of the last trumpet?

The concept was ludicrous in the cold light of day but it wasn't day and that tremendous blast had carried a disturbing medley of sounds. If there was such a thing as the final summons for the dead to rise then it could well have echoed then.

'Over there.' Dumarest rose and strode forward. He halted, waiting until Megan caught up with him with the torch. They looked at a sea of torn and furrowed mud already glistening with heavy frost. 'Further on.'

They moved forward, spreading so as to cover a wider area, their breath pluming in the bitter cold. Twice patches of shadow misled them and then Dumarest felt his foot hit something solid. Together they looked down at a familiar narrow box.

'It's closed,' said Megan. 'The lid — '

Dumarest leaned forward, gripped the lid, threw it to one side.

'God!' said Megan. The torch shook in his hand. 'God!'

A dead woman stared up at them from the depths of the coffin.

She was no longer young, her age accentuated by the dehydrating effects of death. Sunken cheeks made waxen hollows beneath the high bones of her face. The mouth was a thin, bloodless gash. The eyes, open and sunken, looked like murky pools of stagnant water. The arms were crossed on the flat chest. She wore a simple dress which reached from her throat to her ankles. The feet were thin, ugly, mottled with veins.

'He failed,' breathed Megan. His face was white in the light of the torch. 'He carried her all this way for nothing. She didn't come back to life.'

Dumarest was thoughtful, remembering what he had seen. He gripped one end of the coffin, lifted, let it fall with a hollow thud. Leaning forward he gripped the sparse, grey hair. He pulled.

'Earl!' Megan was shocked. His eyes widened as the body lifted. 'What — ?'

It was a moulded shell. It lifted with a faint resistance from magnetic clasps exposing the contoured compartment beneath. A compartment lined with sponge rubber and shaped to hold a woman's body. From it rose a faint odour of perfume.

'Clever,' said Dumarest. He released what he held and it fell back to fit snugly over the compartment. The shell stared up at them, mockery in the muddy eyes. 'The perfect hiding place. Open the box and you'd see what you expected to find — the body of a long-dead woman. There would be no reason to look beneath. Not unless you spotted the difference in weight; that something had gone.'

'Sime wouldn't let anyone touch the box,' said Megan. He lifted his torch. 'Sime! Where is Sime?'

He was gone, vanished into the darkness, leaving nothing but the coffin behind.

13

The guard marched twenty paces, turned, marched back again. She moved with a mechanical precision, breath pluming in the cold air, her footsteps hard on the frozen ground. From the darkness beyond the fringe of light thrown by the torches Dumarest watched, waiting.

'Halt!'

He heard the sharp challenge, the mumbled answer, the sudden commotion. Megan was playing his part well. For a moment longer he waited then, as the guard moved towards the disturbance, raced forward in a blur of speed. He had reached the wall of a tent, crouched, frozen into immobility before the woman had time to turn. A louder noise from where Megan argued with the guards distracted her attention long enough for Dumarest to squeeze beneath the wall.

He was lucky. The room was deserted.

He rose, eyes wide as he searched the

dimness. A solitary lamp cast a shadowy light. A bench littered with instruments of metal and glass stood to one side. Something stirred in a head-high cage and he caught the gleam of watching eyes. Small animals scurried as he moved towards the door. The air stank with the acrid odour of antiseptics.

Beyond the room ran a narrow corridor, equally empty. He stood for a moment, listening, then moved softly down the passage. Footsteps echoed from around a corner and he backed into a room. It was dark, the air tinged with perfume. He tensed as the footsteps came closer.

'One of the travellers, madam. He wanted to see the Matriarch. Naturally I could not allow that.'

'Did he give a reason?' The voice was deep, harsh, impatient. Elspeth, the captain of the guard, was not noted for her tolerance.

'No, madam. He just kept saying that it was important that he should see her. He refused to leave and grew quite heated.' The voice rose, diminished as the speaker passed the room in which Dumarest was hiding. 'I thought it best to call you, madam.'

Elspeth's answer was lost as they turned from the passage.

Dumarest sniffed, inhaling the ghost-scent lingering in the room, hand searching for the light-control. He found it, threw it, hastily reversed it as light stabbed at his eyes. The glare diminished to a faint glow. He saw a small room, painfully tidy, almost bare of furniture. A youth lay asleep on a narrow couch. He turned, mumbling as the light struck his eyes. Dumarest killed the faint glow and stood, waiting, as the man relaxed. Softly he left the room.

And felt something hard grind into his spine.

'Move and I will kill you,' said a hard voice. 'Now turn, gently, and let me see who you are.'

He felt the gun leave his spine as the speaker stepped back, away from the reach of his arms. Slowly he turned and smiled at the physician.

'You!' Melga stared her amazement.

'How did you get here? What do you want?' The gun never wavered in her hand.

'I wanted to test a theory,' he said evenly. 'Also it is important that I see the Matriarch. Will you take me to her, please?'

'Why should I? How did you get past the guards?'

'I sneaked past.' He answered her last question first. 'I wanted to see if it could be done. It can. Now I must see the Matriarch.'

'Why?'

'Because she must know that the safety of her ward is threatened by the Prince of Emmened.' He saw the grim resolution of her face. 'I have just left the tents of the prince,' he explained. 'His physician was kind enough to extend help to those who had suffered from the storm. He is a man who is fond of his wine.'

More than fond, and he had also been loquacious. In Dumarest he had found a willing listener.

'The prince has been affected by the storm,' Dumarest continued. 'He has been interested in the Lady Seena since the fight and was determined to win her. He has left his tents with most of his guards. There can only be one reason.'

'The Lady Thoth?'

He nodded, impatient with her lack of understanding, her apparent careless dismissal of his warning. Then she revealed the reason for her attitude.

'Interesting,' she said dryly. 'Interesting and very ingenious. Your story, I mean.' The gun lifted, centred on his heart. 'But we have seen nothing of either the prince or his guards. No one has entered here other than yourself. And the Lady Seena Thoth is perfectly safe in the company of the Matriarch. Or was — until you came.' The gun gave emphasis to her words. 'Assassin!'

★   ★   ★

He dropped, letting gravity pull him down, using his muscles to jerk him forward and up. He rose beneath the gun, his shoulder lifting her arm, his hands steel traps as they closed on wrist and shoulder. He twisted and the gun fell to the carpet. He doubled her arm behind her back and rested his right hand on her throat, fingers digging hard against certain nerves.

'You didn't fire,' he said calmly. 'I gambled that you wouldn't. Not unless you were certain to hit what you aimed at. The danger of loosing off a weapon in a place like this is too great for you to have overlooked.'

She lifted a foot and tried to smash his kneecap with her heel. He moved deftly to one side and tightened the grip on her throat.

'I could kill you,' he said. 'I could render you unconscious in a matter of seconds. Relax or I may do it.'

'Assassin!' She was wild with fear.

'Fool!' His words reflected his anger. 'You checked me, remember? Don't you trust your findings?'

She didn't answer.

'I came here to see the Matriarch,' he said. 'You can take me to her. Now be sensible and realize that I intend no harm.' He removed his hands and scooped up the weapon. 'Here,' he thrust it into her hand. 'Let's go.'

They checked him first. They stripped him and examined the orifices of his body and only when they were perfectly satisfied did they allow him to dress. Even then the guards were watchful as they ushered him into the inner chamber where the Matriarch sat with the cyber and her ward.

'Dumarest!' The old woman looked her surprise. 'What are you doing here?' He told her, she shrugged. 'The man must have made sport with you,' she commented. 'We have not been disturbed and my ward — ' her hand reached for the slimmer one of the girl ' — has not left my side.'

'No?' Dumarest looked at the girl. She stared back.

'Not since the end of the storm,' she smiled. 'Did you enjoy it?'

'No, my lady.'

'Many did not. Such sounds can all too easily addle a person's brains. There are many dead, I believe?'

'Yes, my lady.' Dumarest sniffed at the

air, the scent of spice was cloying to his nostrils but beneath it, very faint, he could distinguish the perfume she wore. 'And you, my lady. Did you enjoy the storm?'

'It was amusing,' she said casually, then seemed to lose all interest in the visitor. The Matriarch did not.

She studied him from where she sat, tall in the soft lighting which softened but could not remove the stamp of fatigue from the hard planes of his face. The wound on his temple showed livid against the pallor of his skin. His clothes showed traces of mud, the bright fabric dulled by grime. His eyes, she noticed, never left the face of her ward. Inwardly she smiled.

Melga had jumped to the obvious conclusion that he was an assassin — she lacked any other explanation to account for his presence but the old woman knew better. If the physician had never known the power of love she had. And Gath had reminded her of how powerful that emotion could be. Dumarest had come, not to wreak harm, but because he needed to be close.

'Sit,' she ordered abruptly. 'Join us.'

'My lady!' The cyber was quick to protest. 'Is that wise?'

'What is wisdom?' Her face softened with memories. 'Your logic, cyber? Perhaps, but what has logic to do with mercy? The man stays.'

She waited until Dumarest had found a chair and lowered himself into its embrace. She liked the way he sat, remaining poised on the edge of the chair, cat-like in his relaxation. He reminded her of someone she had known, now long dead. The winds of Gath had resurrected his voice and wakened her memory. Now, somehow, Dumarest seemed to make the pattern complete.

'You arrive at an opportune time,' she said, and wondered if he could guess how much she intended to hurt him. Emotional pain, of course, but as deep and as real as any physical agony. 'I am about to name my successor.'

'My lady!'

'Be silent!' She didn't look at the cyber.

'But — '

'Enough!' Her thin voice was strong

219

with anger. Eighty years of rule had taught her how to command. 'It is my will that he stays! My will that he listens!'

She softened a little at the touch of the girl's hand on her own, the firm, young flesh warm against the wrinkled skin. She softened still more as she looked at Dumarest. It was important that he should understand.

'The Matriarch of Kund,' she said gently, 'must forego all the normal pleasures of being a woman. She can have no children. She must not be too attached to any one person. She must devote herself, mind and body, to the good of the worlds she rules. It is a high honour. The position commands vast power and vast responsibilities. The person chosen can have no real life of her own. All she does must be for the good of Kund.'

Her voice fell a little.

'No husband,' she said meaningly. 'No lover. No man to whom she can give her heart. No man whose heart she dares to take.' She paused before delivering the final blow. 'I have chosen my ward, the Lady Seena Thoth, to succeed me as the Matriarch of Kund!'

His reaction disappointed her. He sat, watching the girl at her side, almost as if he hadn't heard a word she had said.

'Do you understand?' She gripped the soft, warm hand so close to her own. 'She, my ward, will succeed me to the throne!'

'Yes, my lady,' he said quietly. 'I understand. But that girl is not your ward.'

He had expected a reaction but its violence surprised him. There was a moment of stillness as if the very air were stunned by the implication, then; 'My lady!' Dyne sprang to his feet.

'He lies!' The girl followed the cyber. Her cheeks were flushed, her eyes bright with anger. She threw herself at Dumarest her fingers reaching for his eyes. He rose, gripped her wrists, flung her back against her chair.

'Guards!' The old woman knew how to handle an emergency. As the women poured into the room she snapped a terse command. 'Hold!'

She waited until the guards had closed

on the others ready to grip or strike should the need arise. Irritably she sniffed at her pomander. The drugs were too weak. She needed something stronger to sharpen her mind and strengthen her voice. She found it in her anger.

'You!' She rose and glared at Dumarest. 'Explain!'

'My lady!' The girl was oblivious of her guards. 'How can you allow such a man to insult me? A penniless traveller to make such an accusation. Men have died for less!'

'As he will die if he cannot prove his statement,' promised the Matriarch. She stared at Dumarest, her face cruel. 'It will not be an easy death, that I promise. Now, explain!'

'Yes, my lady.' He paused, looking at the girl, the cyber, the watchful guards before looking back at the old woman. 'I can only guess at your reasons for coming to Gath,' he said. 'But I would imagine that one of them was to arrive at a decision concerning your successor. Would that be the case?'

'You digress!' snapped the old woman,

then, 'Yes, that is correct.'

'It would not be hard for a man trained in the arts of prediction to guess whom that successor would be.' Dumarest did not look at the cyber. 'Almost anyone, knowing you, your attachment to your ward, knowing too of this journey could have made a similar guess. The worlds of Kund are rich, my lady?'

'Very.'

'Such a prize would be worth a great deal of trouble. That trouble was taken. If the successor of your choice could be replaced by a tool of their own — what then of the worlds of Kund?'

He paused, conscious of the heat of the room, the scent of spice, the rising tension. Conscious, too, of the narrow path he trod. The girl had been quick to point out their relative positions. Had the Matriarch been of the same nature as the Prince of Emmened he would be dead by now. But she, of all people, could not dare to make a mistake.

'Continue!' She held a golden pomander to her nostrils, it muffled her command.

'A man named Sime arrived on the

same ship as the Prince of Emmened. With him travelled a crone and a man little more than a boy. Sime carried a coffin in which reposed the dead body of his wife. Or so the crone told those who were curious. They believed her, why not? Gath is a strange world with strange potentialities. It was natural for him to have carried such a burden to such a place.'

'Why?'

'As a disguise. How else could a tall young woman, attractive, regal, be shielded from view? You were alert, watchful for assassins, wary of anything you could not explain or trust. Once your suspicions had been aroused the plan would certainly fail. But there was nothing to arouse your doubts. A man with a coffin. A poor, deluded creature more mad than sane. How could anyone guess that, beneath the outer shell, rested the twin of your ward?'

'You lie!' The girl lunged forward, sobbed with frustrated anger as she felt the restraining grip of her guards. 'My lady! He lies!'

'Perhaps.' The Matriarch put aside her pomander. 'If so, he will regret it. Continue!'

'The crone was working with Sime. It was she who told the story, circulated the rumours, watched the coffin while he slept. The young man travelled with them by chance. She killed him during the storm. She tried to kill me in the same way but failed. Now she is dead.'

Dead at the bottom of the cliff, driven over the edge by the confusion of the winds, dead and taking her secrets with her. Muscles knotted at the edge of his jaw as he thought about it.

'The rest is simple,' he rasped. 'At the height of the storm the substitution was made. The Lady Seena was lured into a quiet room. This girl had been smuggled into the tents. They changed clothes and the impostor answered your summons. She stands at your side. The person who you would make the next ruler of Kund.'

He fell silent, waiting, guessing what the questions would be.

'An ingenious fabrication,' said Dyne in his soft modulation. 'You will note, my lady, how much has been glossed over. The Lady Seena lured into a quiet room. The supposed impostor smuggled into the tents. How?'

'I penetrated your guards,' said Dumarest. 'What I could do, almost unaided, others could do far easier with help.' He looked at the Matriarch. 'I found the empty coffin. In it, below the empty simulacrum of a dead woman, is a hollow compartment. The girl rested there drugged with quick-time. She left the scent of her perfume. I smelt the same odour in a room belonging to the cyber's retinue. The girl is wearing it now.'

'My perfume?' She was bold, he had to give her that, but how else could she be? 'You must know it, my lady. It is a scent I always wear.'

The old woman nodded.

'And how does he know so much?' The girl was triumphant. 'He is lying, my lady. He had no reason to suspect Sime. How could he?'

'Because I am a traveller,' snapped Dumarest. 'I know how they act, how they feel, how they are after a passage. No genuine traveller could have carried that coffin from the ship. Sime realized his mistake and asked for help. He got it. But later, when I offered him a lift for his coffin, he refused it. That box was heavy, I know, I helped to carry it. Sime was a fake.' He saw the expression in the old woman's eyes.

'I have met others of his type before,' he said quietly. 'They look gaunt, starved and almost dead but they are far from that. Their muscles are more efficient, their metabolism a little different, that is all. Your physician will verify that. Sime was no experienced traveller. My guess is that both he and the crone bribed the handler and rode High. Their companion had to die to seal that knowledge. The stakes were too high for them to take any risk.'

'And you?' The old woman was shrewd. 'Why should they want to kill you?'

'I don't know,' he admitted. 'Perhaps because I had been close to the Lady Seena. Perhaps because someone wanted me dead. I think the crone shot at me on the journey but I can't be sure. I am sure

227

that she tried to kill me during the storm.'

'So you say,' said the Matriarch. Then, 'Is that all?'

'Yes, my lady.'

He knew that it wasn't enough.

★ ★ ★

The Matriarch thought the same but the seed of doubt had been planted and she had to be sure. Unerringly she asked the one question he couldn't answer.

'Where is this man Sime?'

'I don't know, my lady.' He added to the answer. 'He is not with the other travellers. I saw no sign of him by the coffin. He could be making his way back to the field or — '

'Yes?'

'He could be hidden in your tents.' He realized the emptiness of the suggestion. 'I doubt that he is but — '

'Search the tents!' snapped the Matriarch to her guards. 'Send outside to find the coffin and bring it within.' She returned her attention to Dumarest. 'You claim that this girl has been substituted

228

for my ward. Now, if she came from the coffin, as you claim, where is my ward now?'

The cyber gave him no chance to answer.

'Surely that alone proves the fallacy of his claim, my lady. Assuming the logic of what he says there could only be one place where the real Lady Seena could be hidden. Inside the coffin. I assume that he has not found her?'

'No,' said Dumarest shortly. Then, 'I have no doubt that she was supposed to be hidden in the coffin after the substitution. No doubt either that Sime, still acting his part, would pretend grief and rage and throw it over the cliffs into the sea.' His eyes met those of the Matriarch. 'It would be the only safe thing to do,' he explained. 'The coffin had to be as it was. The weight had to be the same in case anyone was curious. And there would be no need to keep the Lady Seena alive longer than was essential.'

'I am the Lady Seena Thoth!' The girl screamed her rage. 'Remember that!'

'Quiet, child.' The old woman was

disturbed. The traveller made good sense assuming that he knew what he was talking about and he had never struck her as a fool. But one thing troubled her. 'Why? Why have you bothered to tell me all this? What is Kund to you?'

'Nothing. But your charity saved my life after the fight with Moidor. I like to pay my debts.'

She nodded. 'Then prove what you say.'

It had come to the critical point as he knew it must. Suspicion wasn't enough. Her fingerprints and retinal pattern would have been tailor-made to match, the rest of her physique the same. The substitution must have been planned for years — those responsible would have made no obvious mistakes.

'During our journey,' he said slowly, 'we left the rafts and wandered towards the east. We stood watching and you likened the column to something. What was it?'

'A snake.'

'Nothing else?'

'Perhaps, I can't remember. The

conversation and the company were not that important.'

'And neither is this test,' said Dyne. 'Without witnesses what can it prove?'

Nothing, of course, her word was as good as his and Dumarest recognized defeat. But he had to try.

'After my fight with Moidor. You summoned me and we sat talking. It was just before the phygria attacked. You remember?'

'Of course.'

'Yes.' He wondered who had briefed her. It had been thoroughly done. 'We were talking. About a friend of mine on Quail. Something reminded me of him. What was it?'

'My ring.' She held out her hand to show it gleaming on her finger. 'You said that the ladies of Quail used them for sport. They filled them with powerful aphrodisiacs.' She yawned. 'Your friend suffered from their sense of fun.'

'That's right,' said the Matriarch. Her face was hard as she looked at Dumarest. 'If she were not my ward how would she have known that?'

How?

'No, my lady,' said Dumarest softly. 'That isn't the question. The real question is how do you know it?'

He watched the answer dawn on her face.

14

The mirror! She turned to where it stood then hesitated with instinctive caution. It would not amuse her ward to learn that she was a target of a spy-device; amuse her still less to know that the knowledge was shared by the common guards. But that, at least, could be prevented.

'Leave us,' she snapped at the women. 'Wait outside.'

The room seemed larger when they had gone.

'You!' She pointed at the girl. 'Stand back. Right back against the wall.'

'My lady?'

'Do as I say!' The old woman relaxed a little as the girl obeyed. Now, if she were careful to shield the mirror with her body, not even her ward need know of its secret.

'My lady!' The girl was insistent. 'What other proof can I give?'

'A moment, child.' The Matriarch's

voice was soft but determined. 'We shall soon know the truth.'

Dumarest watched her as she turned. He frowned, not understanding what she was about, then he saw the old back stiffen, the withered hands clench in a paroxysm of rage.

'You!' She turned, her face distorted, her eyes burning with anger. 'You liar! Guar — '

The girl was quick. She sprang forward and to one side, her hand lifting, levelling, something spurting from the ornate ring on her finger. It shrilled across the tent and buried itself in the Matriarch's side. She fell, gasping, still trying to summon her women.

'Guards!'

Dumarest shouted as the hand swung towards him. He ducked, throwing himself forward, flesh cringing to the expected impact. None came. Instead there was a sudden vicious snarl and the stench of burning. Dyne stood, a tiny laser in his hand, the dead body of the girl at his feet. A charred hole in her temple told of the accuracy of his aim.

'My lady!' Elspeth thrust into the room at the head of her guards. Her eyes narrowed, grew dangerous as she saw the Matriarch writhing on the floor. 'Who —?'

'Get Melga!' Dumarest thrust her aside as he stooped over the old woman. 'Hurry!'

The thing the girl had fired shrilled its deadly vibrations, boring deeper into the flesh, destroying cell, nerve and tissue with its lethal song. Dumarest snatched at it with his left hand, tore it free, flung it aside. Smoke rose from where it fell on the carpet, a ring of flame circling a widening spot of ash.

'A vibratory dart,' said Dumarest as the physician knelt beside him. 'I may have got it out in time.'

Melga pursed her lips as she examined the wound. Deftly she fired a pain-killing drug into the Matriarch's throat. Resetting the hypogun she fired three charges of antitoxin around the pulped place where the dart had struck. An antiseptic spray to cover the raw flesh with a healing film completed her immediate treatment.

'Show me your hand.' Her lips pursed even tighter as she examined Dumarest's fingers. They were dark, bruised as if caught in a slamming door, the tips seeping blood. The blast of her hypogun terminated their pain.

'Dumarest!' The Matriarch stared at him, her eyes haunted hollows in the withered pattern of her face. Shock had closed the iron hand of age. She swallowed, weakly, gestured for him to come closer. Her voice was a thin reed of sound. 'You were right,' she whispered. 'That girl is not my ward. She must be made to tell what she knows.'

'The girl is dead,' he said shortly. 'Dyne killed her.'

She nodded, fighting the lethargy of the drugs, able to concentrate only on the thing of greatest importance.

'Seena,' she whispered. 'You must find her and bring her back safely to me. Find her and . . . ' Her voice trailed like smoke into silence.

'My lady!' He reached out, tempted to slap the sagging cheeks, to shock her into awareness. Instead he touched her gently on the shoulder and steeled his voice. 'My lady!'

She blinked into his face.

'The Lady Seena,' he urged. 'Do you know where she is?'

'You will find her,' she said. 'You promise?'

'Yes, but — ' He sighed as she yielded to the soporific effects of the drugs.

* * *

The Prince of Emmened was insane. He tittered as he walked and sang snatches of ribald song interspersed with crude verse and cruder oaths. The ground rang iron-hard beneath his feet, frozen by eternal night, locked in the stasis of ice. Cold caught his breath and converted it into streaming plumes of vapour.

'The gods are kind,' he chuckled. 'They spoke to me from the wind and told me the thing I must do. Can you guess at what that is?' He looked at her, sidewise, his eyes very bright.

'No,' she said dully. They had given her a cloak and a scarf hugged her head but her shoes were thin and her feet frozen.

'They told me to follow my star.' He ran a few paces forward, faced her, his face mad in the light of the torches held by his guards. 'You are beautiful, my lady. So very beautiful.'

She didn't answer.

'So soft and warm and full of fire,' he continued falling into step beside her. 'Crowder said that.' He laughed at amusing memory. 'Crowder is dead, did I tell you? He listened and went quite mad. He thought that he was his own father and flogged himself to death.'

Again she remained silent. He scowled as she made no response.

'I am not used to being ignored, my lady. I have ways to deal with those who so displease me.'

'You remove their tongues,' she said. 'I have heard the rumours.'

'Then you had best beware.' He laughed again, enjoying the situation. 'Some would say that a dumb wife was a thing to be envied. Such a one would never be able to tell of things which should remain secret — or send lying tales to that old bitch of Kund!'

'Of how you stole her ward in the height of the storm?' Seena did not look at the prince. 'I have told you before — you will regret it.'

'Perhaps. But have you considered, my lady, I could have saved your life?'

He was too near the truth for comfort. Numbed, knowing that she had been drugged but helpless to do anything about it, she had allowed Sime to take her out into the storm. She remembered the look on his face when the Prince of Emmened had appeared out of the darkness. His relief when he learned that the prince intended to abduct the girl. The nightmare journey when she could only follow the insane ruler. The journey was still a nightmare but now she could move of her own volition, speak her own mind. Neither movement nor speech was enough to save her.

Perhaps guile could.

'The Matriarch will thank you for what you have done, prince,' she said. 'Return me to her, unharmed, and you will have a friend for life.'

'I don't want a friend!' He was petulant, dangerous in his anger. 'I have many friends and can buy more.'

'No, my lord.' She sensed his rage and guessed its cause. The fury of the storm had ruptured delicate cells in his brain. His physician, unlike Dyne, had not made provision to combat the harmful vibrations.

'You say 'no'!' His good-humour had evaporated. 'How long will it be, my lady, before you change your tune?'

'Are you tired of me so soon, my lord?'

'No. Never that!' His eyes glowed as he looked at her. 'You know, my lady, it is time I settled down. You would make an excellent wife. You shall make an excellent wife. Soon we shall arrive at the field. A ship will take us to Emmened. Elgar can take care of things on Gath. By the time he rejoins us you will be well on the way to providing me with an heir.'

She remained calm. She had guessed what was in his mind from the beginning.

'Well?' His eyes searched her face. 'Does not the prospect please you?'

'Yes, my lord.'

'It does?'

'Of course, my lord,' she lied. 'You are rich and powerful and a handsome figure of a man. Why should I object to becoming your wife?'

He smiled at her, his good humour restored. He leaned close, his breath wreathing her face, the vapour stinging as it turned to frost.

'A hundred men shall fight to the death to celebrate our mating,' he murmured. 'I shall garland you with entrails and let you hack the living flesh from shackled slaves. Our passion will be fed with pain. The worlds will have reason to remember our union until the end of time.'

She smiled despite the crawling of her flesh. He was quite insane.

★ ★ ★

'The nightside.' Dumarest stared at the scene depicted in the mirror. The girl, the prince, his guards seemed like tiny manikins, their shadows dancing in the pale glow of torches. A creeping chill seemed to seep from the frame.

241

'Are you sure?' Melga frowned her puzzlement. 'Surely, if he wanted to abduct her, he would have made for the field by the shortest route.'

'Perhaps he is,' said Dumarest shortly. 'Or perhaps he hopes to throw us off pursuit. This mirror gives us an advantage. The point is — how do we stop him?'

He looked from the physician to the captain of the guard. Elspeth had a stubborn set to her jaw.

'The Matriarch must be protected,' she said flatly. 'That is my first duty.'

'Agreed. But you have spare guards?'

'A few.'

'Then send them to the field. They are to travel at a run. If they arrive before the prince they are to stop him and rescue the Lady Thoth no matter what the cost. Is that understood?'

She nodded, glaring at him as if tempted to deny his right to give orders, then she swung from the room and Dumarest could hear her hard voice rapping commands. The physician shook her head.

'They won't make it in time,' she said. 'The prince has too great a lead.'

'Perhaps.'

'You said they might be taking a shorter route,' she insisted. 'And, even if the guards do arrive in time, what can they do? They are outnumbered.'

'They can fight.'

'And die,' she agreed. 'But will that save the ward of the Matriarch?' Her eyes probed his face. 'You have a plan,' she said. 'Tell me.'

'You have supplies of slow-time?'

'Yes.' She guessed his intention and her mouth set in a stubborn line. 'No,' she said. 'You can't do it. The risk is too great.'

'I accept the risk.' He met her eyes, his determination matching her own. 'I know what I'm doing. It's the only possible way to catch them in time. Now get me the drug.' His face darkened as she hesitated. 'Hurry, woman! Or is the drug of greater worth than the girl?'

The insult was undeserved. He knew it and apologized when she returned. Her flush told of her appreciation.

'You said that you knew what you were doing but few have used slow-time in the conscious state. The dangers are too great. It isn't just a matter of living faster, you know.'

'I know.'

'I hope that you do.' She handed him a small bag. 'These glucose tablets might help. You're going to need all the energy you can get. Unconscious you'd be no problem, I could supply intravenous feeding and your energy-demand would be relatively low. Conscious — ' She broke off. 'Well, you know about that. Just remember that the square law comes into effect on food requirements and about everything else.'

'I'll remember.'

'You'd better.' She looked down at the hypogun gleaming in the light. 'What I'm really trying to say is that you must be very careful. Do you understand?'

He nodded.

'All right. But just remember to take things slowly. Slowly!' She raised the hypogun and aimed the blunt snout at his throat. 'Good luck.'

She pressed the trigger.

He felt nothing, not even the air-blast carrying the drug into his bloodstream but, with shocking abruptness, the universe slowed down. It hadn't, of course. It was just that his own metabolism, reflexes and sensory apparatus had suddenly began operating at almost forty times the normal rate. The danger lay in accepting the illusion of a slowed universe as a reality.

He moved from where the physician stood poised on the balls of her feet, the hypogun still in her hand, her finger hard against the trigger. The light seemed dull, tinged with a pronounced reddish cast and the tiny figures depicted on the mirror-screen had frozen into rigid immobility.

He stepped to the door and pulled aside the barrier. The thin material moved reluctantly as if made of lead. He stepped through, passed an immobile, vacant-eyed guard, reached the outer door. The material was thicker, heavier, he strained for minutes before it would move. Ducking through the opening he walked

245

from the tents to the plain.

Steadily he began to walk towards the nightside.

A wind rose about him as he walked, roaring past his ears, building up into an almost solid wall of air against which he stooped fighting the hampering restriction. The ground felt soft beneath his feet, the stars reddish points in the sky.

Suddenly he tripped and fell, drifting down like a feather but hitting the ground with savage force, jarring his bones and ripping a patch of skin from the side of his face. He lay gasping from the shock, cold with the fear of injury. Climbing to his feet he examined the ground, noting the deep indentation made by his foot, the equally deep but much longer gouge torn by his falling body. The wind had stopped and gave him the answer. He had hit the ground with the impact velocity of about fifty miles an hour. Only fantastic luck had saved him from serious injury.

Cautiously he continued his journey.

He ate as he walked, sucking at the tablets of glucose which were strangely hard and slow to release their energy. He had plenty of time to think. He was living at about forty times the normal rate but could not walk at a normal speed. A normal speed, for him, was over a hundred miles an hour but at that speed wind resistance made progress impossible. His clothes too presented a problem. His speed had increased but not his strength and he felt as if he were clothed in lead. The inertia of his garments aided the wind in slowing him down to a steady thirty miles an hour.

It was fast enough. It was ten times the travelling speed of a party moving over rough and unfamiliar ground and he would catch up with the prince even allowing for time wasted in search and following barren trails.

Ten times as fast — but he needed more than ten times the energy to do it.

In slow-time a man would starve to death before he had a chance of growing old.

15

The room was very quiet, the lights soft, the air tainted with the odour of antiseptics beneath the comforting scent of spice. On a pneumatic mattress the Matriarch rested, almost mummy-like in her immobility, the withered pattern of her face. Bandages swathed her side and drugs coursed their slow way through her blood. She felt no pain, no trepidation, only a peculiar detachment as if her mind were divorced from her body so that she could ponder events with an objective viewpoint.

She was thinking of Dumarest and what he had said.

He had known nothing of the mirror and its secret so why should he have been so interested in discovering how she had learned of what had transpired between himself and her ward? He had meant something unconnected with the mirror. He had seemed to be trying to give her a message. He —

She opened her eyes and stared at Dyne. 'My lady.' His voice was smooth, his face, his very clothes. He stood at the foot of the bed, tall in his scarlet, his cowl throwing shadow across his face. A machine of flesh and blood uncontaminated by emotion. And then she remembered.

'You!' Her voice was a whisper. 'You knew what had taken place between them. You could have told the girl.'

'My lady?'

'You were with me watching in the mirror. Just before the phygria attacked. You — ' She broke off, seeing the pattern as it fell into place, each piece fitting to make an incredible whole. 'It had to be you. No one else could have arranged for the exchange. No one else could have told her all she needed to know. You!'

He said nothing, waiting.

'You killed her,' she whispered. 'After she attacked me you killed her. You had to keep her silent for your own sake. Alive she could have told too much.' Her hand scrabbled on the coverlet. 'But why? Why should you, a cyber, engage in such intrigue?'

His eyes were cold, relentless, his face

as if carved from marble.

'Power? Wealth? Personal ambition?' She whispered the motives which drove normal men into such actions and knew that none of them could apply. The cyber was not a normal man. 'But you failed!' she said triumphantly. 'You failed!'

'Because of Dumarest,' he admitted. 'Because of an unknown factor. I told you once, my lady, that I was not infallible. Always there is the unknown element to take into consideration. But, if it had not been for the traveller, your ward would be dead and her substitute your successor to the throne of Kund.'

'Is that why you tried to kill him? You must have primed the phygria — or told your agents to do it. They must have tried to burn him on the journey and stab him during the storm.' She paused, chest heaving, cold with the knowledge of how close he had been to success.

'The mirror,' she whispered. 'You would have changed the setting but I gave you no opportunity. You had no time. Dumarest exposed the plot before you could do the one thing which would have proved him to be a liar.' Her mind spun with the unanswered question. 'But why? Why?'

He had no intention of giving her the answer. The plans of the Cyclan encompassed the universe and rulers were merely pawns to be moved according to the great design. The Lady Thoth was independent and had no love for any cyber. Her substitute, prepared years ago, was amenable and, better, utterly predictable. More he neither knew nor guessed.

'I shall ruin you!' Anger stiffened the thin voice. 'I shall expose you and your Cyclan for what you are. Never again will you be trusted.' Her hand lifted, trembled as she pointed. 'Go!'

'No, my lady.'

'You dare — ?'

'If you shout your guards will not hear you.' He touched the bracelet around his wrist. 'A cone of silence surrounds us. But you will say nothing, do nothing. If you do then I will be impelled to divulge certain facts about you and your ward. The fact that you and she are blood-relations, for example.'

'You lie!'

'No, my lady. The girl is the daughter of your grandchild — the one you placed in a position of safety when you accepted the throne of Kund. She should have been killed. No Matriarch of Kund is permitted to have natural issue and you know the law. Instead you took the throne and kept both your romance and its issue a secret. Now you intend to make her your successor. If the truth became known that would not be permitted. And it is the truth — I can prove it.'

He paused, looking down at her.

'Your silence for mine, my lady. It seems a fair enough exchange.'

She was helpless to do other than agree.

★　★　★

The Prince of Emmened was hopelessly lost. He stood in a circle of his guards and cursed them, the fates, the lack of guidance and everything but himself. They were too cold to argue, too afraid to do other than huddle together for mutual protection. Around them the cold gripped the soil, threw streamers of frost over icy boulders, made even the dancing shadows things of menace.

'Move!' screamed the prince. 'Move! Move!'

His words came as dull, rolling echoes to the man above. Dumarest leaned against a boulder and stared down at the bobbing lights, the immobile men. He was tired with a bone-aching weariness that numbed his mind and made even the hunger clawing at his stomach seem insignificant by comparison. He had walked countless miles against the never-ending pressure of strength-sapping wind, following false trails, circling the area, climbing and slipping and clawing his way over rock and ice. He had fallen, ripping his clothes and bruising his flesh, so that his face was a mask of blood and dirt. Now, at last, he could rest.

But not for long.

He jerked awake from the edge of sleep, sucking great gulps of air to clear his mind, wishing that he could feel some of the cold of the region. Instead he sweltered in the generated heat of forty times normal living. It did nothing to help him combat the fatigue of days of travelling without rest. It was hard for him to realize that he was only hours normal travelling from the plain.

Below the circle of men had moved a little, perhaps a step or two. They did not look up as he scrambled down towards them. They remained motionless as he circled, looking for the girl. He found her, a huddled bundle of misery, her feet white with frostbite. Beside her the prince, face twisted, mouthed his insane filth.

Dumarest poised his fist.

Sense came almost too late. He twisted, venting the force of his blow on the empty air, feeling sweat bead his forehead at the thought of what he had almost done. His fist, travelling so fast, would have crushed the prince's skull — but would have shattered itself to ruin at the same time. That was not the way.

He stooped and picked up a stone. It felt as heavy as lead, rising slowly from the ground, hanging poised as he aimed

254

it. He threw it with the full strength of shoulder and arm directly at the skull of the prince.

Before it hit he was beside the girl. He saw the impact, the slow unfolding of flesh and bone and spurting brain. He stooped and slowly, very slowly, picked up the unresisting body. It was stiff, unyielding, feeling as if made of wood but he knew better. Care was needed to avoid bruising the tender flesh, snapping the delicate bones. As blood began its slow pulse from the headless trunk he was walking from the dead prince and his unsuspecting guards. The wind of his passage was the only sound he heard. The ice was his only danger.

The ice and his own fatigue.

He walked, towards the end, in delirium. Faces swam towards him from the starlit gloom, voices whispered from the wind of his passage, each boulder seemed to hold a snarling enemy, each twist of the path a cowled figure intent on his death. It was a long time before he realized that someone was calling his name.

'Dumarest! Dumarest! What's the matter with you? Dumarest, answer me!'

It was the girl. He looked down at her, a leaden weight in his arms, and saw her lips move, the breath vapouring above her mouth. Even as he watched it grew still and the wind of his passage droned again past his ears.

He was coming out of slow-time but not as he would if unconscious; a single step from fast to normal. The dying effect of the drug was erratic, his overstrained metabolism swinging to its stimulus.

'Dumarest!'

He heard the voice and spoke quickly while he had the time.

'It's all right. You're safe. The prince is dead and I'm taking you home.'

'Dead?'

'Quite dead.'

'I'm glad,' she said. 'He deserved to die. You killed him, didn't you?'

Dumarest didn't answer.

'You killed him and saved me.' Her voice was soft, warm, promising. 'You won't regret this. Yooo . . . o . . . o . . . o . . .'

Her voice slowed, deepened, ground to

a stop as again he jerked into accelerated living. Ahead the mountains cut across the sky. They jerked closer, closer, dipping and swaying as he stumbled towards them. A part of his mind told him that he was being a fool, that he should slow down, take things easy. There was no need to hurry now that they were safe. Enemies didn't lurk in every shadow, crouch behind every boulder. Fatigue and his abused metabolism were combining to induce delirium.

Then, in the shadow of the mountains, his delirium became real.

★   ★   ★

'Dumarest!'

He heard the voice and saw the shape, tall, cowled, the scarlet black in the cold light of the stars. It stood before a wall of rock, dark against the shimmer of ice. He looked down. The girl was asleep or unconscious, he couldn't tell which. He stooped and gently placed her on the ground. He rubbed his arms as he rose to face the cyber.

'I should have known,' he said bitterly. 'Your breed are clever at laying traps and snares.'

'I predicted that you would be here at this time, yes,' said the cyber. 'It was a simple matter. Remain still!' he snapped as Dumarest moved a little. 'Do not move.' He stepped forward, the laser in his hand accentuating his command. He glanced down at the cloaked figure. 'How is the girl?'

'Unconscious.'

'It is as well. There is no need now for her to die.'

'Are you sure about that?'

'I am sure.' Dyne stepped back to his original position. 'You are surprised? But then you are a creature of emotion not of logic. The Cyclan does not waste time on the futility of revenge. The past is irredeemable. We are interested only in the future.'

'I am glad to hear it.' Dumarest swayed, fighting the fatigue which threatened to engulf him. He felt a brief hope as wind roared past his ears but it was a natural gust not the result of accelerated living. Now, when he needed it most, the effects of the drug seemed to have left him. 'Sime is lying dead a short way from here,' he said. 'The prince must have killed him. I found his body on my way out.'

'And the prince?'

'Dead.'

'Yes,' said Dyne. 'He would be.' Starlight splintered on the rising barrel of his gun. 'As you will be.'

'Why?' Dumarest took a slow and cautious step aside and away from the girl. 'Why must you kill me? Because I exposed your plot? I thought you regarded the past as irredeemable.' He took another slow step. 'Or is there another reason? Is it because I come from a planet called Earth?'

'What do you know of Earth?'

'I lived there. I spoke of it and you must know that. I think that you want me dead because of it. What is so important about Earth that no one must speak of it?' He took another cautious step.

Dyne followed him with the gun.

'You are trying to distract me,' he said.

'You hope to approach and then, suddenly, attack. You have confidence in the speed of your reflexes but they will not save you. When you reach a certain position I shall fire.'

Dumarest drew a deep breath.

'Earth,' he said. 'A lonely world with a strange form of life. Underground life, cyber, do you understand? I escaped on a ship serving that life and it bore a device similar to the one you carry on your breast. The Cyclan Seal.'

'So?'

'I think that perhaps you could tell me how to find that world. You or those like you.'

'You are talking to gain time,' said Dyne. 'The reason eludes me. There seems to be neither logic nor sense in your actions and yet you must have a motive. It can only be to gain time. Therefore I will kill you now.'

His finger closed on the trigger of his weapon.

★　★　★

Wind screamed from the east. A vestige of the dying fury of the storm, whining through the pass, roaring against the ice-clad rock, pressing invisible fingers into hair-fine cracks. Something cracked high above. Dumarest heard it even as he flung himself from the lancing beam of the laser. A thin, high, splintering against the blast of the wind.

'Dyne!' he yelled. 'Dyne!'

The cyber turned, the wind pressing the cowl hard against his face, blinding him with the sheer material. He tore it away from his eyes, saw Dumarest, aimed his weapon.

A second crack came from above. It sounded loud against the dying wind, the yielding of ice from its rocky bed, the grinding rumble of its fall. The cyber heard it. He looked up as a shadow dropped from the stars, helpless, the gun forgotten in his hand. Dumarest heard it, saw it fall, was leaping forward as it caromed from the wall of rock to shatter harmlessly to one side.

He'd had the advantage of perspective but that was all. It had to be enough.

He grabbed for the cyber's gun hand, locking his fingers around the wrist, smashing the hand against the rock until it released the weapon. Pain tore at his nerves as Dyne kneed him in the groin. He twisted his head aside barely in time to save his eyes from stabbing fingers. He tasted blood as a fist tore at his throat.

Desperately he fought for his life.

The cyber was strong, trained in the mechanical skills of destruction, cold in his deliberate efficiency. Dumarest was weak, worn out with lack of sleep and continuous effort. But he had one advantage the cyber lacked. He could feel hate and fear and the burning need for survival. He could let his instincts and reflexes take over from his conscious mind, letting the smouldering fury of his subconscious lend him a temporary strength. He grabbed Dyne's throat and dug his fingers into the flesh beneath. He kept them digging while blows rained on his body. He dug them in as the blows grew weaker, slower, finally ceased. When, after a long while, he released them, the cyber was dead.

'Dumarest!' The sound of the falling ice had wakened the girl, that and the animal-noises of combat. She lifted herself on one elbow, staring at the crumpled shape, the pale face white beneath the shadow of its cowl. 'Dumarest!'

'It's all right.' He stood swaying over her, sucking great gulps of air into his lungs. When the world had stopped spinning he stooped, picked her up, cradled her in his arms. 'He's dead. It's all over.'

'Dead?'

'He died in the storm.'

It was true enough, and it would serve to keep the Cyclan quiet. His racing thoughts outmatched the slow progress of his feet. The girl was vague, suffering from cold and exposure, unaccustomed to hardship. But she would live, and might even be grateful. The Matriarch would certainly be.

It could be an advantage to have powerful friends.

They could even help him find his way back home.

Home! His face hardened as he thought about it. Well, he had a clue now. Better than the vague, half-remembered thing he'd had before. Dyne had confirmed his suspicion that the Cyclan had connections with Earth. One day, perhaps, he would add to that knowledge.

He stumbled and almost fell, suddenly conscious of the ache of his body, the fatigue tearing at the last vestiges of his strength. Well, that could be cured too, given time and the skill of the physician.

He paused as he neared the tents of the Matriarch, a freak action of the drug suddenly accelerating his metabolism. A gust of wind swept down from the mountains and he heard the music of Gath.

Deeper now, slower, but quite unmistakable.

The empty sound of inane, gargantuan laughter.

THE END

We do hope that you have enjoyed reading this large print book.

Did you know that all of our titles are available for purchase?

We publish a wide range of high quality large print books including:
Romances, Mysteries, Classics
General Fiction
Non Fiction and Westerns

Special interest titles available in large print are:
The Little Oxford Dictionary
Music Book, Song Book
Hymn Book, Service Book

Also available from us courtesy of Oxford University Press:
Young Readers' Dictionary
(large print edition)
Young Readers' Thesaurus
(large print edition)

For further information or a free brochure, please contact us at:
Ulverscroft Large Print Books Ltd.,
The Green, Bradgate Road, Anstey,
Leicester, LE7 7FU, England.
Tel: (00 44) **0116 236 4325**
Fax: (00 44) **0116 234 0205**

Other titles in the
Linford Mystery Library:

CALL IN THE FEDS!

Gordon Landsborough

In Freshwater, Captain Lanny was an honest cop with problems: his men and his chief were on the take from the local gangster Boss Myrtle. Bonnie, Myrtle's daughter, was in love with Lanny, but he couldn't pursue the relationship because of her father's criminal activities. Lanny's problems multiplied as Freshwater became threatened by an influx of murderous criminals from New York — a gang of bank raiders, and Pretty Boy, a psychotic murderer of young women. Then Bonnie went missing . . .